REACHING DEEP

~~~

Four Stories

by

Jon Etheredge

REACHING DEEP
Copyright © 2012 by Jon Etheredge
All rights reserved.

Fedoro's Jump
     First edition, July 2011

Avalon Fires
     First edition, July 2011

Shooter Two-Two-Three
     First edition, April 2010
     Second edition, July 2011

Coward's Song
     First edition, April 2010
     Second edition, July 2011

STORIES

Fedoro's Jump

Shooter Two-Two-Five

Avalon Fires

Coward's Song

Fedoro's Jump

ONE

Maggie Fedoro made toast and coffee, typical fare for a Saturday morning. She hadn't felt like cooking in weeks, so she cooked bacon and country ham and apple turnovers, too. Then she made grits, because you can't really enjoy country ham without grits, everybody knows that. The grits needed butter, and next to the butter was a package of sharp cheddar cheese, so she made omelets, whipping the eggs with cream and soda water, and serving them in the center of the plate on top of the wheat toast.

"Just coffee for me, thanks."

"Alvin, love of my life, do you know why most women convicts are in prison?" Maggie placed his plate on the table and pulled out his chair.

He sat down and jammed a piece of bacon into his mouth. "Somebody ought to call Raleigh Flight Service and get a real forecast before we head out."

"Somebody should stop whining and enjoy breakfast. The weather's gonna be fine. Here's your coffee, and the phone is right over there. You can call the weather man yourself, if it's so important."

"I wasn't thinking about me." He took a tiny bite of the country ham.

"Oh, of course not!" she laughed.

"No, really. It's the newlyweds who're jumping this morning…"

"Relax, I'll tell the newspaper to photograph your good side."

"Hey, look, I need good winds or I can't drop 'em, and if they don't jump today I don't get paid ..."

"Oh, stop it. They'll jump," she said. "I think you're more worried about your ten-way."

Alvin quit nibbling and put the slice of ham back on his plate. "I've been skydiving for nearly twelve years," he said. "Now I'm two jumps shy of a thousand and it's a weekend and the weather is perfect..."

"...And you're a perfect wreck. Tell me something...why does jump number one thousand have to be a ten-man star? Why not just do a hop-n-pop and get it over with? You'd still get a certificate and a free beer."

"Because it's special, that's why, and I want a party."

"Darlin', you're *payin'* for the party. It's not fair. Money's tight right now."

"Fair has nothing to do with it. Technically, the Loggins...Largins...the newlyweds are payin' for the party." He cut into his omelet.

"Laarzens," she said. "Tell me you haven't forgotten their names, again."

"It's difficult!"

"Laarzen. C'mon, say it. L-a-a-r-z-e-n."

"L-a-a-r-z-e-n."

"Your mind is stuck, that's all. You'll do OK once you get 'em into a plane. How high are you guys gonna go for the ten-way?"

"Five thou."

"Five? You're gonna try to finish a ten-way in only twenty seconds? I'll give you this much, you're the most ambitious husband I've ever had. Tell me the newlyweds' names again."

"L-a-a-r-z-e-n. George and Tina..."

"Wrong genders. Georgina and TeeJay. Say it."

"Georgina and TeeJay L-a-a-r-z-e-n."

"Look, I'll remind you about their names when we get to Good Hope. Don't worry, dear. I won't let you look like a *complete* fool."

"Appreciated," Alvin said, chewing his last bite of toast. "Oh, the time! We gotta get our gear ready."

"Your gear, not mine, I'm not jumping today. *Delicate condition*, remember?" She patted her belly. The morning sickness was still holding off so far, but she wasn't going to risk barfing inside a plane.

"Well, you could help me pack out."

"Uh-uh. No heavy lifting. I got a doctor's note."

"Walk with me, then…"

Maggie cradled her coffee with both hands and held the front door open with her foot. Alvin lugged four heavy canvas satchels with all his skydiving gear down the stairs to the parking lot, hefting them one by one into the back of their old Ford pickup.

Maggie walked back into the apartment building.

"We need to get going!" he shouted.

"Don't yell," she said leaning out the kitchen window on the second floor.

"Hey, what's the answer?" he yelled again.

"The answer to what?"

"Why are most of the women convicts in jail?"

"They poisoned their husbands."

TWO

The drop zone at Good Hope was not much to look at from the ground. A badly maintained side road led to a brown clay parking area that used to be covered with gravel. Three metal pipes stuck up vertically through the ground, marking the edge of the airfield. The pipes were the only reminder of a stout fence that used to keep cars from driving directly onto the flight line.

The fence had been a bad idea. Cars needed to drive onto the flight line every now and then, and the jumpers didn't appreciate being told their moral integrity demanded a lockable gate. One fine, drunken Saturday afternoon, they fixed their little fence problem with a ten-pound sledgehammer.

The flight line was a grassy field, tightly mown and wet with the dew of a cool May sunrise. It was the center of the airport and served as the landing zone, packing area, and taxiway. The field's dirt strip, hidden in the pines, was blanketed in a low fog.

Mike Street had his name embroidered over his left breast pocket. On the opposite side were the words "Chief Pilot" and "Operations Officer". No one argued about the titles, since Mike owned both of the skydiving planes and had paid the hangar rent mostly on time for the last five years.

Ordinarily, he would have enjoyed the quiet solitude of his morning runway walk-down, listening to the creak of pines and the rustle of unknown animals grazing at the edge of the dirt airstrip. But today, Rudy Jackson showed up early to help with the walk-down.

Rudy was a distraction. He wouldn't stop talking. His chatter sucked all the Zen out of the runway inspection and made Mike forget that it was his turn to make coffee.

"Rudy, you're dumping bad vibrations all over my morning. What's on your mind?"

"Oh, hey, Mike, like... um, I was wondering if maybe I could get some twin-engine time today."

"In the Beech?" he snorted. "I don't think so, lad. The old girl's much too delicate to let the likes of you touch her sensitive parts."

"I can handle it," Rudy said. "I fly the 180 pretty good, don't I?"

"Time will tell. I still have to pull the heads to make sure you're not shock-cooling the engine."

"Mike, I know what I'm doing in that plane. I come down fast, but I always put in a few extra inches of manifold just to keep the temp up."

"You do OK."

"I do better than OK. You've seen me fly. I can usually beat the last jumper to the ground."

"A Continental 470 engine ain't the same thing as a radial 985, and the Beech 18's got two of those."

"It's nothin' I can't learn, Mike."

The chief pilot stopped in his tracks and put his fists on his hips, what his wife called his "thinking pose". He tucked his chin against his chest and, a moment later, squeezed his eyes tightly shut, surrendering.

"OK, Rudy. We've got two lifts scheduled today. You fly the newlyweds in the 180 and then jump into the 18's left seat. I'll let you handle the takeoff, we'll do the climbout and drop together, and then I'll do the descent."

"Thanks, Mike. You won't be sorry."

"You're right about that. The rest of the day you'll pay off the flight time in the Beech by driving the 180 for no pay." Mike turned and marched off into the hangar to preflight the big Twin Beech. Rudy grinned and sprinted to the little Cessna 180, parked on the grass apron in front of the gas pump.

Tony Torrino, the jump club's treasurer and official Signer of the Checks was hammering tent stakes into the short grass next to the hangar prior to laying out his repacking mat. "Hey, Rudy, got coffee yet?"

"Nope! It's Mike's turn to make it."

More jumpers arrived within minutes. They laid their packing mats side-by-side around the edge of the field, grumbling and demanding coffee. A few had already stretched their main canopies and were busy arranging shroud lines and snapping air into the gold and red and blue panels, kaleidoscopes of nylon that didn't need to be repacked, but it never hurt to double-check and be sure.

Rudy was bent over the Cessna 180's cowl, his arms buried up the elbow trying to check the engine oil. The dipstick had been getting harder to pull out and today it was firmly jammed, defying Rudy's most insistent pulling and cursing. Across the field, every jumper heard it break free and slam into the top of the cowl with an unmistakable *PopBangDammit!*

The 180 was an old plane and an even older design. Instead of a wheel under the engine, it had a small swiveling wheel beneath the rudder. It was tricky to control on the runway, like pushing a shopping card backwards, but it handled rough ground better. The seats had been removed to save weight, so the jumpers sat on the bare metal floor, waiting their turns to exit. Getting in and out meant crawling and scooting, a slow and uncomfortable process.

The pilot's seat was a skeleton framework of welded tubing, made to hold a canvas sling instead of a cushion. The perpetually tangled seat belts were bolted to the floor and the shoulder harnesses were soaked in oil and sweat. They smelled bad even in a high wind so Rudy never used them.

A man and a young, attractive woman, strangers on Good Hope's field, caught everybody's attention. They disappeared into the open hangar, followed by a prim middle-aged lady carrying a camera and a small notebook.

Mike Street was watching the coffee maker work when the trio came into the office. "Excuse me," the man said, "we're looking for Alvin Fedoro. He's our instructor..."

"...*jumpmaster!*" the young woman corrected. "He's our jumpmaster."

"I'm TeeJay Laarzen," the man said, shaking Mike's hand. "This is Georgina, my wife."

"Hi, I'm Mike. You guys must be the newlyweds," Mike said. "Alvin isn't on the field, yet, but I can offer you some coffee while you wait."

Tony Torrino stuck his head inside the open hangar door. "There's coffee?"

"No. Get lost, Tony."

In the distance, the fading echo of a single word rippled across the field. "Coffee!"

TeeJay looked around and found a usable cup, but by that time the pot was empty. Georgina had been looking at the faded photographs on the office wall and was fully distracted by one of the few framed pictures. It was a glossy print in full color, showing ten skydivers locking arms in a star formation. The photograph was taken from above the group and gave a sharp, clear view of each man's helmet, harness, pack, boots and butt crack.

"Say, Mike. What's the story behind this?" Georgina asked.

Mike came over and looked at the picture. "They're naked," he told her.

"That's rather obvious," she said. "Why?"

"Why what?"

"Why are they *naked?*"

"Um...I don't remember."

TeeJay called his bluff. "C'mon, Mike. What's the story?"

"OK, but you didn't hear it from me. That's Alvin Fedoro's five hundredth jump. He wanted something special. That's him right there," Mike said, pointing at a nondescript pair of biscuits.

Georgina giggled and asked, "How can you tell?"

"That's his rig. See the knife right there? Alvin's the only guy I know who carries a knife laced into his harness."

"Looks cold," Georgina said.

"Stick around," Mike said. "Alvin's doing it again after you guys jump. This afternoon he's making jump number one thousand. They're gonna be making a ten-man star, just like the one in the photo."

"Will they all be naked?" TeeJay asked.

"I don't know about the others, but Alvin probably will be."

The Lady with the Camera had an idea. "Let's get some pictures inside the plane," she said, pointing at the Twin Beech. "They'll give the article some depth. TeeJay can sit in the pilot's seat and Georgie can put on a parachute and pose by the door."

"Yeah, lady, that would be great." Alvin Fedoro dropped his equipment bag just inside the hangar door, its thud echoing off the hangar walls. He walked over to greet the newlyweds and told the Lady with the Camera, "Except that's not the right plane. Hello, Georgina... TeeJay."

Maggie had reminded him of their names as soon as they had parked.

"Don't listen to Mike, here. He's a liar. I've got jump suits and helmets in the bag. Why don't you grab some coffee and find something that fits and I'll meet you over there." He pointed at the Cessna 180.

"Ain't any coffee," Mike said.

The Lady with the Camera interrupted, "Can't they use this plane, instead? It's bigger. We can go along and watch the jump."

"That plane's reserved for a special group going up after the Laarzens land. Mike, what do ya mean there ain't no coffee? Is the machine broken?"

Mike was standing at the door to the Twin Beech, digging in his pockets. "Oh, *hell*! I can't believe this...locked." He walked outside the hangar and yelled for Rudy.

"What?" Rudy was standing on the 180's tire, checking the fuel level in the wing tank.

"The Beech is locked and I don't have the keys! Watch the place while I go home and get 'em, will ya?" Without waiting for an answer, he hurried out of the hangar.

"Can you bring back some coffee?" Alvin asked, but Mike was already too far away to hear the request.

Georgina was the first to get coveralls on. They fit like bloomers and the legs were much too long, so Alvin knelt down and rolled the cuffs up. A few seconds later, TeeJay was ready, too.

Georgina wrinkled her nose at her husband, "You smell funky!"

"It's not me, it's the suit."

Alvin sniffed the air between the newlyweds and said, "Yeah, well sometimes they don't make it into the washing machine until later. Try not to think about it. Let's head over to the plane."

Tony Torrino passed going the other way for a coffee refill. "Hey, Alvin. I dropped your chute bag off at the plane, man."

"Thanks, Tony. I owe ya."

The Lady with the Camera got to the Cessna ahead of Alvin. She was leaning over the right wing spar, taking a snapshot of Rudy Jackson through the open jump door, while he sat in the pilot's seat. Alvin overheard them talking as he walked up.

"What did you do then?" the Lady with the Camera asked.

"Not much I could do with a broken leg. I dragged myself back uphill to where the plane had impacted and pulled my passenger out of the wreckage just before the wing tanks…"

"Hi, Rudy." Alvin stuck his head in the door. "Plane ready?"

"Yeah, she is… 'cept we need gas. The tanks are about a quarter full, but the pumps are locked."

Alvin jiggled the large, expensive padlock that secured the nozzle to the pump and asked Rudy for the keys.

"Mike went home to get 'em."

"Jeez, Rudy! He could be gone an hour."

"It's been a half hour so far. He should be back pretty soon."

"Well, I can burn up a little time with a student run-though. Can I borrow the plane for a final briefing?"

"Sure," he replied. "Just call when you're ready to go up."

Alvin pulled two parachutes out of the gear bag, one for each of the Laarzens. He reached in and pulled out a third student harness, one without a static line, for himself.

"This is how you put the parachute on." He showed them how to balance the pack while pulling the saddle deep under their thighs. He hooked the reserve packs to the fronts of their harnesses, and explained the automatic openers. "We'll arm your reserves only when we're above a thousand feet," he told them.

"OK, final practice. Everybody in the plane." Alvin said. "TeeJay, you're first out, so let the missus get in first." One by one, they each scrambled along on the floor of Cessna 180 while the Lady with the Camera snapped shots of each move.

"Just like you learned in class," Alvin reminded them, walking each one through a practice jump. It was just practice, so he didn't hook up their static lines. There would be plenty of time to do it for real when they were in the air.

Alvin pointed at TeeJay and then at the platform. "Sit in the door!" he said loudly. TeeJay slid along the floor and let his legs dangle outside, inches from the grass.

"Stand up!" TeeJay grabbed the strut and pulled himself into a hunched over "ready" position, both feet on the jump platform.

"Go!" Alvin pounded TeeJay on the shoulder with the flat of his hand. TeeJay pushed himself backward off the platform, holding his arms out and back.

"COUNT!" Alvin shouted.

"One thousand *one*... one thousand *two*... one thousand *three*..."

"Look up!"

"Canopy OK," TeeJay said.

"No, it's not…look again. *Lineover*!"

TeeJay went through the motions of pulling his reserve ripcord. Satisfied his student might survive the jump, Alvin turned and pointed at Georgina, still jammed uncomfortably in the back of the empty fuselage. "Sit in the door!"

The Lady with the Camera clicked away from a low angle that made it look as though the young bride were actually jumping, except for the bright yellow static line that was clearly attached to nothing. Oh, well. At least she had a few good shots of the practice.

Alvin shouted for the pilot. "Rudy… *Rudy*! Let's go, we're ready."

Rudy jogged to the Cessna from the office. "Mike's not back, yet," he said.

"So what? Let's go."

"Can't…we need gas."

"How much fuel does she have right now?"

"About an hour, give or take."

"That's enough for one drop," Alvin said.

Rudy thought it over. Normal procedures called for topping off the tanks before the first flight. But it wasn't actually written anywhere, and it wasn't a regulation or a law or anything. Besides, two student drops and Alvin's "hop 'n pop" would take twenty to thirty minutes at the most. He'd refuel when he got back and then hotfoot it over to the Beech for some multiengine time.

"OK. Just don't blame me if we run dry and crash."

"Why not? Aren't you the pilot in command?" Alvin joked.

Georgina and TeeJay had already loaded up and were scrunched together in the back of the cockpit. Alvin sat with his back to the instrument panel and swung his legs inside. As Rudy climbed into the pilot's seat and fumbled for his seat belt, Maggie appeared in the jump door with a kiss for Alvin.

"Don't break nuthin'," she said.

Rudy called out, *"Clear"*. A split second later the prop spun twice and the engine roared to life. Maggie pushed the jump door closed and waved "goodbye" to the newlyweds. She walked back to the office as the Cessna taxied down the runway. She didn't watch the takeoff. Morning sickness took priority. "This won't take long," she thought.

THREE

The pilot's headset muffled the screaming growl of the Cessna's engine but the jumpers had no such protection. Talking was impossible. Rudy watched the altimeter, tapping Alvin's shoulder when they climbed through one thousand feet.

Alvin switched TeeJay's automatic reserve opener to "Armed". A small explosive cartridge would jerk the reserve parachute open if his main parachute failed. Alvin signaled to Georgina to sit tight. He would arm her reserve later.

Rudy pulled the throttle back and the Cessna leveled out at twenty-five hundred feet, the jump altitude. Alvin unlatched the Snohomish door and the wind pulled it out of his hands, holding it up against the bottom of the wing. The air blasting through the open door was cold and immediate, startling the newlyweds, waking them up, and forcing them to pay attention.

Alvin shifted his weight and knelt by the door, his head sticking out into the slipstream. He focused intently on the ground below, visualizing the track of the plane and guiding Rudy across the center of the drop zone.

The track was good. One minute to go. Alvin pointed at TeeJay and signaled him to scoot closer. He reached around behind the groom and pulled out the first four feet of his static line, hooking it to a steel ring welded to the airframe.

Alvin checked the ground track one more time, turned to TeeJay and shouted as loud as he could, "SIT IN THE DOOR!"

TeeJay barely heard the command, his eardrums assaulted by wind and fear and a pounding heart, but he slid forward anyway and forced himself to sit on the edge of the door. His legs dangled out into an eighty-mile per hour wind that threatened to pull him out of the airplane feet-first. The fear whipping him was solid and insane and normal. He looked back at his new wife. Georgina was watching. Georgina wanted him to jump. It would be the manly thing to do.

"STAND UP!" Alvin shouted, pointing at the small jumping platform covering the right-hand wheel. TeeJay reached out, grabbed the strut, and pulled himself outside the safety of the plane, his feet barely balanced on two square feet of doom.

Below, everything was green and brown, jumbled and meaningless. The wind slipped beneath TeeJay's goggles and made his eyes water, blinding him. The recycled football helmet on his too-small head threatened to fly off at any second. He had never heard a wind so loud, so insistently reminding him that he was not yet prepared to hurl himself into the arms of the afterlife.

Less than two feet away, Alvin sat in the door, looking down as they approached the drop zone. His right hand rested on TeeJay's left shoulder, a small reassurance that someone in this world still cared whether he lived or died. Peeking around the corner of the jump door was Georgina, his wife, his beloved, his beneficiary, smiling with the lips of an angel – lips puckering dryly for the kiss goodbye, the final kiss, the smooch of the damned.

He didn't dare move. His thighs started to cramp. His mind screamed for an excuse to crawl back into the plane.

"GO!" Alvin shouted, slapping TeeJay's shoulder.

The groom's feet took one step back and the rest of him tried to catch up, arching his body as he had done in the classroom. The sensation of falling overtook every thought, leaving nothing but the primal need to scream. It lasted forever. He couldn't think. He couldn't breathe. His chest pounded and his arms flailed and his legs kicked at empty air. Only when he felt the soft deceleration of his parachute opening did he remember to count.

Alvin watched TeeJay fall thirty feet and stop, safe and happy under a perfect parachute. He pulled in the loose static line and signaled Rudy to go around one more time.

FOUR

On the drop zone, Maggie clicked her stopwatch as soon as she saw TeeJay's canopy open. In another minute he would be crossing the automatic reserve altitude.

She clicked the transmit button on her walkie-talkie and held it to her mouth. "TeeJay, this is Maggie. If you can hear me, kick your legs." A second later, the tiny silhouette of the student flipped his legs back and forth like a swimmer.

There were more than twenty people on the ground at Good Hope, some of then non-jumpers, a few beginners, and several with hundreds of jumps to their credit. Everybody stopped what they were doing and turned their heads upward to watch the first jump of the day.

Satisfied that he could hear her, Maggie turned her attention to bringing him down safely. She clicked the transmit button again. "Turn your automatic opener off. Kick your legs when you are done."

High overhead, the Cessna rolled level on its second jump run.

FIVE

Alvin signaled Georgina to slide closer to the door. As he armed her automatic reserve, he felt Rudy tap him on the shoulder. He turned around and saw the pilot pointing at the fuel gauge. Both tanks were showing close to empty. Rudy held up a single finger and yelled, "*One pass!*"

Alvin quickly pulled out the bride's static line and hooked it to the frame of the pilot's seat, making sure to lock the latch before pointing at the jump platform.

"STAND UP!"

Georgina grabbed the strut and swung out onto the platform in a single smooth movement. There was no sign of anticipation or fear. She was grinning. She was ready.

"GO!"

She arched gracefully and let the wind wash her off the plane. One, two, three… three seconds of freefall were over too soon. Then the parachute canopy blossomed and she became heavy in its harness, slowing almost to a stop more than half a mile up.

Alvin waited until he saw Georgina under a good chute. Then he saluted the pilot and dove out the open door, his hands clapped together in a parody of a high diver. He planned a ten second freefall, opening his chute a little low but getting back to the coffee pot quicker.

Rudy felt the plane yaw to the right a little bit. Not much, but he didn't like it. The jump door was still open… maybe that was the problem. He pulled on the closing cord and the door snapped down easily, but when he let go, the door flew open again.

He tried twice more and both times the door refused to latch closed. Rudy looked around and saw the problem, stretched across the plane's metal floor.

Alvin had forgotten to pull the last static line back inside before diving out. Rudy leaned over and pulled on the nylon strap with his right hand, but it wouldn't move. He had heard of this happening, static lines getting caught up on an antenna or snagging the landing gear.

Alvin was going to be mad, but Rudy had no choice. He had to cut the line. He reached for the survival knife that was duct taped to his shoulder harness.

Dammit! The knife was gone! Unbelievably, somebody must have needed it more than he did. There'd be hell to pay when he got back on the ground, yessir, and that was going to be pretty damn fast! Rudy chopped power and pulled the flaps all the way down. In a hurry to get on the ground while he still had a little gas, he pushed the Cessna's nose down into a steep diving turn.

SIX

Maggie saw the second canopy open and started her stopwatch again. Then she saw Alvin tumble out of the Cessna. He'd probably drop down to under two thousand feet before opening his chute. She knew he'd be in a hurry to get down.

Except he wasn't coming down. He wasn't going anywhere at all. He was just sort of... flying formation? No, that wasn't possible.

She peered through the binoculars again and fought the nausea that welled up inside. Voices around her gasped.

"Something's wrong..."

"Look... who is that?"

Alvin was hung up on something. He was tied to the Cessna, backwards, flying next to it feet first, his arms loosely flapping. And then something changed. The plane started a spiraling dive. Rudy was coming in for a landing.

"Oh my God." She turned and screamed, "MIKE! *MIKE!*"

Mike was still preflighting the Twin Beech when he heard Maggie scream something about a radio. He looked up in time to see her throw the walkie-talkie to one of the ten-way jumpers and sprint into the hangar. "OhGod... ohGod... ohGod..." she panted, running past him and into the Beech 18's open jump door.

"Maggie, what the hell..."

"...Radio! I need the radio!" She stumbled as she forced her way to the cockpit, hit the master power switch and pulled the headset on at the same time. The Twin Beech had old avionics. It was several seconds before the radios were "hot."

Radio number one was already set to the field Unicom frequency. The other plane should be listening on the same channel.

Maggie keyed the microphone. "Rudy! Rudy, do you hear me?" She released the transmit button and heard a moment of static.

Then, Rudy's voice. "*Affirmative, Maggie. Turning short final.*"

She screamed into the microphone, "NO RUDY! GO AROUND! For God's sake, GO AROUND! Alvin is hung up under you." She waited for acknowledgement. Rudy didn't answer. The Cessna was in view, now, sliding into a high-speed final approach a hundred feet above the trees at the end of the runway.

SEVEN

Jerking painfully to a stop was just a piece of the puzzle that Alvin's muddled brain was trying to put together. The wind was another piece. He knew that he was upside down. A powerful hand gripped his right ankle, pulling him through the air as fast as the airplane next to him.

"*Airplane?*" he thought. "*I'm snagged on something.*"

Blood rushed to his head. His groin muscles were torn on the left side. His right foot was throbbing and the knee on that side was shot through with white-hot pain. He tried to look at his legs, but couldn't see past his reserve parachute. Mounted on his chest, the pack blocked his view.

Alvin twisted, struggling to unsnap the reserve. It took him a few seconds, but when he finally freed one side, the prop blast ripped it from his hands. Half-connected, the fist-hard reserve chute flailed in the wind and smashed into his jaw. Alvin made a panicky grab at the swirling pack and missed, its rigid frame chopping him across his face, closing his left eye with a swollen, cut eyelid. He was losing the fight. The wind made it impossible to reconnect the pack to the harness. He had to get rid of it.

Alvin tried to catch the pack again, but it whipped flat against his face, cutting his upper lip and bloodying his nose. Ignoring the pain, he unhooked the last buckle and groaned in relief as the reserve parachute fell away and the beating stopped.

He looked at his feet. A stout yellow strap – Georgina's static line – was triple-wrapped around his right leg, just below the calf. He reached around beneath his left arm for his emergency knife, only to discover that it was safely laced onto his other harness, safely packed away in the truck, waiting for his special jump.

The Cessna's engine slowed to idle and Alvin heard the electric flap motor whirring. The horizon was tilted crazily to the left, and he knew instantly that Rudy was flying a steep-angle approach back to the field.

With renewed urgency, Alvin searched his jump suit pockets, his boots, even his helmet, hoping for a miracle in the form of a knife – any kind of knife.

He was inwardly astonished at how calmly he was taking all this. Tied to the plane, invisible to the pilot, he was going to be dragged to death as soon as the plane touched down on the runway. Alvin took a deep breath and asked God not to let it hurt too much.

He kicked his right foot, but the line held tight. He cursed and twisted, and tried pushing the fouled static line off his right ankle with the sole of the left jump boot, but that only made the knot cinch down tighter. He needed a damn *knife*.

The trees were so close! Couldn't the people on the ground see him? The ground was rushing past him faster.

The Cessna made its last turn and lined up with the runway. Even if a knife suddenly materialized in his hands, even if he managed to cut through the thick static line, Alvin realized that his parachute would never open at this height. There was no more time.

His thoughts were calm and beyond the reach of panic. The plane was below the treetops now, starting to flare for the landing. In seconds, he'd be dead. He wondered whether Maggie was watching. He hoped not.

Alvin asked God's forgiveness.

EIGHT

Maggie watched helplessly from the Beech 18's cockpit as the Cessna disappeared below the trees, its nose lifting to flare for landing.

"Rudy go around, Rudy go around, Rudy go around," she repeated mechanically into the microphone. A second later, the old Cessna flew by the field at the midway point, fifteen feet off the ground, its engine roaring at full power, Alvin still tied to the static line.

Rudy's calm voice rang through the Beech's radio. *"OK, Maggie, I'm going around. Say again about Alvin... is he down already?"*

Maggie's voice came alive again. "Rudy, Alvin is hung up... trapped under the 180. Get back up into the pattern and stand by."

Rudy leveled off at eight hundred feet, the altitude for the landing pattern. He leaned over to his right and tried to see outside the jump door, but his seat belt kept him locked in place. Defying the Federal Aviation Administration and the law of gravity, he unbuckled his seat belt and let it clatter to the floor.

He eased himself off the pilot's seat and edged close to the jump door. The Cessna detected the weight shift and dropped its right wing. Rudy hurried back onto the seat and dialed in enough rudder trim to compensate for his movement the next time.

Grabbing the frame of the seat, he slowly leaned out the open jump door. The plane felt the center of gravity move, but the new trim setting kept the wings level. This gave Rudy a few extra seconds to absorb what he was seeing.

Ten feet beyond the edge of the jump door, Alvin was hanging by one ankle. The static line had somehow fouled itself around his leg and was now tied tight. His face was bloodied and his reserve parachute was missing.

Rudy climbed back onto the pilot's chair and radioed the drop zone. "Maggie, is Mike with you?"

"*Rudy, Mike here.*"

"Alvin's hung on a static line. I can't reach him and I got no knife."

After a moment's silence, Mike came back on the air. "*Rudy, what's your altitude?*"

"Eight hundred."

"*Climb to five thousand.*"

"I don't know," Rudy said. "Fuel's nearly empty."

"*What? On one flight? How's that possible?*"

"Mike, I couldn't get any gas… you had the keys."

"*You damn well should've waited! Now you've…*"

~~~

Maggie pulled the microphone away from Mike's mouth and pried his thumb off the switch. "Dammit, Mike! Fight later! Right now what do you say we *save Alvin!*"

Mike nodded. "Rudy, stay at eight hundred and circle. We're coming up." Then he turned to Maggie and told her, "Go get Tony. I'll meet you on the runway."

Maggie dashed out the Beech 18's open door, yelling Tony's name at the top of her lungs while Mike hurriedly started the left engine. The plane lurched forward on one motor, and the right propeller started turning as soon as the plane's tail cleared the hangar door.

Tony was gawking at the Cessna and the silhouette of the man hanging beneath it. Her voice brought him to attention. "*Tony!* C'mon! Alvin's in trouble!" The big Twin Beech taxied behind her, heading across the field. Maggie caught up to it in a dead-out run and launched herself through the open door.

Tony paused along the way to scoop up his parachute. He reached the Beech's open door just before they got to the runway. Sprinting alongside, he threw his skydiving rig into the plane. Then he grabbed one of the handles mounted outside the door and swung his body into the plane like a gymnast.

"What's the problem?" Tony asked Maggie, trying to control his breathing rate at the same time. Before she could answer, an oak barrel in a yellow jump suit flew in through the door and collapsed painfully on the steel deck.

"Hey, Boats," Tony said. "Glad you could make it." 'Boats' was Boatswain's Mate First Class Luther Springdale, USN, more than a mere man and a good person to have around in a bar fight.

Maggie climbed uphill to the cockpit and told Mike, "We got people on board. Get me up there *now*."

"Yes, Ma'am."

She hurried back to the two men in the back and filled them in on what was happening, shouting to be heard over the two huge engines. "Alvin is hung on a static line under the 180. He can't get loose and Rudy doesn't have a knife."

The Beech spun around, pointing down the runway, and Mike fed gas to the hungry radial engines on each wing. In seconds, they were airborne.   Tony hurried into his parachute harness.

"Why doesn't Alvin cut it, then?" Boats asked.

"I don't know," she answered.

Mike throttled back and the change in sound alerted the three people in the back that they were getting close. Maggie held onto the safety bar over the door and leaned out as far as she could. They were pulling even with the Cessna 180. Alvin saw them and waved weakly.

Tony stood in the center of the door and pointed directly at him, then pointed at his own foot, and then stiffened his right hand and made a cutting gesture across his left arm. Alvin read the message clearly, *"Cut yourself free."*

In response, Alvin patted his chest, his hips, and his back pockets. Then he shrugged. "*No knife.*"

Tony held up one hand, showing Alvin his palm. "*Wait.*" Then he turned to Maggie and Boats and pointed at the cockpit. The three of them trundled up through the cabin and huddled close to Mike.

"We need to get him a knife," Tony said. It sounded so reasonable and simple. Everybody on board had a pocketknife, and there was a Navy surplus survival knife in a sheath bolted to the side of the jump door. All they had to do was to get it to a man thirty yards away.

Mike was the first one to state the obvious. "Sonny, how are you plannin' to get it from *here* all the way over to *there*?"

Tony took a long look at the Cessna off their left wing. It wasn't flying steadily. Instead, it bobbed up and down. The only idea he could come up with was suicidal. But it was, after all, the only idea.

"Long line," Tony explained. "Tie a rope to me and drag me over there. I'll take the knife to Alvin."

Mike shook his head. "You'll kill yourself and everybody in that plane. No. It's nuts."

"How much line do you need?" Maggie asked.

Tony quickly figured the angles and said "At least a hundred feet."

"Well that kills it," Mike said. "We don't have any rope."

Boats leaned in and said, "Yes, in fact, we do."

He reached around and jerked Tony's ripcord. The container popped open and the parachute spilled out onto the Twin Beech's floor, a mass of nylon and cotton and zigzagging shroud lines. Twenty-four shroud lines, each one fifty feet long and strong enough to hold more than five hundred pounds.

Before Tony could object, Boats opened his KaBar folder and sliced off all but four lines on each side of the harness. He cut and spliced line after line, folding and knotting them into a finished rope. Within five minutes, Tony's parachute had been sliced into trash, but now he had seventy feet of white nylon rope tied to his harness.

"It'll hurt when you hit the end," Boats warned. "Can't be helped. We'll guide Mike into position. You just cut Alvin loose real fast, then cut away yourself." He folded his KaBar and dropped it into the leg pouch on Tony's jump suit.

Maggie pulled out her Gerber and zipped it into the shoulder pocket of Tony's suit. "You'll need this more than I will," she said.

Boats looped the makeshift rope into the now empty chute deployment bag, and attached the bag to Tony's main pack. "It'll pay out neater," he explained. With the last ten feet, he tied the rope to a deck hitch. "Maggie, go forward and relay my directions. We're gonna fly ol' Tony here right into Alvin's lap!"

Maggie shot him a thumbs up and hurried back to the cockpit.

"SIT IN THE DOOR!" Boats shouted to Tony, showing him how to hold his arms so the rope wouldn't break his neck as it snapped tight.

"GO!"

Tony gave a little hop and was instantly clear of the door. His body turned lazily in the Beech 18's propeller wash as he fell and fell faster and then snapped to a stop at the end of the makeshift rope.

It didn't hurt like he thought it would. The nylon shroud lines stretched a little, softening the blow at the bottom. Some of Boats' knots couldn't take the strain and snapped like guitar strings. But when the fall was over, there were still three intact lines on the right riser and two on the left.

Boats leaned out and checked on Tony. He was behind the Beech and about thirty feet below it. Tony was sailing like a kite, his body arched and his arms pulled behind his back. Skydiving horizontally, he was able to go up and down, but side-to-side movement was difficult. He looked up and saw Boats watching him. Tony pointed at the Cessna impatiently. *"Let's go there!"*

~~~

Alvin thought he was having a pain dream. It looked like someone jumped out of the Beech and got caught at the end of their line. "*Just like me*," Alvin thought. "*No, not exactly like me. That guy is hanging heads-up. Is that Tony?*"

The Beech drifted back into position behind and slightly above the Cessna. Slowly closing the distance with the smaller plane, the Beech bobbed about lazily. Mike was having trouble flying in formation with Rudy. Alvin's brain was still drunk but it looked to him as though the people in the other plane were going to try to actually land on the Cessna.

"*Why is a man hanging from that long rope?*" he wondered.

The Beech roared overhead, dragging a human being close behind it. Alvin recognized Tony Torrino and waved at him. Tony kept moving forward, grabbed at the Cessna's wing and missed. The Beech didn't stop in time, pulling Tony too far, dragging him directly over the Cessna's propeller.

NINE

Looking up, Tony saw Boats watching the other plane and signaling to Maggie. She was sitting in the cockpit, relaying Boats' orders to the pilot. Mike's corrections were late. Tony suddenly realized that the plan wasn't going to work.

The Cessna was directly beneath him. He saw Alvin give him a little wave and got ready to descend for the rescue. But something was wrong. He wasn't slowing down. Mike hadn't reduced power soon enough. Tony shrugged at Alvin and got ready for another try.

He looked up and saw Boats frantically signaling for Mike to back off. But instead of slowing down, the Beech started a slow descent, lowering Tony into the Cessna's spinning prop.

Sandwiched between the two planes, Tony helplessly watched the razor-sharp prop arc get closer. He thought it might be a joke and would tell Mike exactly how he felt about it, except it wasn't a joke. The Cessna's propeller was getting closer and the joke was over. The aluminum blades were spinning directly at his chest.

Acting out of pure instinct, Tony stuck his arms out in front of him. The edge of the round blur touched Tony's left hand. Almost painlessly, his outermost two fingers were nipped off at the second knuckle.

Tony barely had time to register the loss, spinning halfway around and leaving him upside down, his back to the deadly arc, waiting for the final blow. He closed his eyes and was making his final peace when he realized that his death was taking too long.

Tony opened his eyes and twisted around for a look below him. The Cessna was pulling forward slowly, descending, opening a gap wide enough for a full and productive life.

Above him, Tony saw Boats waving wildly, trying to get his attention. As Tony watched, Boats formed a knife with his hand and drew it across his throat - "*Cut away.*"

"*No!*" Tony shook his head. Then he held up the index finger on his left hand to signal for one more try. The hand was strangely slick and red, and was two fingers too narrow.

Boats gestured again, "*Cut away.*"

Tony knew he was right, but he also knew Alvin didn't have any options. Leaving his friend to die alone carried a sting that would never go away. One hand on each shoulder, he gripped the canopy release loops.

Everybody heard the same sound at the same time. The Cessna's exhaust sputtered and quit dead, the fuel tanks dry. The decision to abandon his Alvin was no longer in Tony's hands.

He waved "goodbye" to Alvin and pulled down hard on the canopy releases. Almost instantly, he fell away from the rope that had tied him to the Twin Beech. A plain white parachute streamed out of Tony's reserve pack, popping open with a canon-like boom five hundred feet above the ground.

Still trapped in the bight of a wayward static line, his right knee in white-hot agony, Alvin Fedoro laughed.

TEN

Rudy felt the engine go dead. He didn't pause to think about what to do next. Every pilot knows what to do. Training takes over. Rudy pushed the nose down to set up the glide. Within a second, he had started a gentle turn that would line him up on the runway.

"HEY!" It was Alvin's voice.

"ALVIN! WE LOST POWER!" he shouted back.

"I'M STUCK!"

"I GOT NO CHOICE. I GOTTA LAND."

"I'm still STUCK," came the distant response.

"I'M GONNA PUT IT DOWN ON THE GRASS. NEXT TO THE RUNWAY, ALVIN – ON THE TALL GRASS NEXT TO THE RUNWAY!"

"How high… HOW HIGH ARE WE?" Alvin yelled.

"SIX-FIFTY. ALVIN, I'LL BE AS GENTLE AS I CAN."

Alvin knew that touching down at fifty miles an hour would be lethal, even on the grass next to the runway, even on lamb's wool. This was a helluva way to complete jump number nine hundred and ninety-nine – great jump, crappy landing!

"SIX HUNDRED."

Alvin didn't want to hear a countdown to his own death. He tried kicking the side of the Cessna, but his free leg had a torn groin muscle and wouldn't move. He tried to tell Rudy to shut up and just land and get it over with, but he no longer had the strength to shout. After a moment's contemplation, he lost his temper and elbow-punched the Cessna's thin aluminum skin, making a barely noticeable dent in the metal.

"FIVE HUNDRED."

Alvin thought about the baby Maggie was carrying. They hadn't talked about a name, yet. They didn't know whether it would be a boy or a girl. That had to wait for her doctor's appointment on Monday. No, she'd have to reschedule – Monday would be his funeral. What would Maggie tell their child about Dead Daddy? That he died having fun? That he was a good man?

"FOUR HUNDRED."

Alvin could make out the individual leaves on the trees below. It wouldn't be long, now. He wondered who they would blame. The static line looping around his leg was just bad luck, that's all. In a year, that's all anyone would remember. Yeah, *"Good old Alvin... bad stroke of luck that... let's have another beer!"*

"THREE HUNDRED. ON FINAL, ALVIN!"

Alvin had an epiphany, that he was frightened more by pain than by death. It was a waste of time, therefore, to worry about whether his death would hurt. Of *course* it was going to hurt. He suddenly had an option, an alternate path. There would be pain, and he'd probably die anyway. But so long as he accepted the pain, he had a chance.

"TWO HUNDRED. HANG ON BACK THERE!"

Alvin pulled his ripcord.

It was over in a second. The parachute canopy opened behind him, seizing the air and stopping his body like an anchor. Tied to his leg by the static line, more than a ton of airplane jerked on the other end at a hundred miles an hour, fighting for the prize. Alvin knew what would happen next. The weakest link between the parachute and the Cessna 180 would fail.

He was ready for the shredded cartilage, the ripped tendons and veins, his bones being torn apart. He had accepted the unavoidable, the pain beyond agony, beyond perception. Surprisingly, all he felt was a sharp, uncomfortable snap. It reminded him of stories he had heard of shark bite victims losing a foot or an arm or a whole leg, but feeling nothing more than a tug.

ELEVEN

The Good Hope Volunteer Fire Department dispatched "Rescue 7", their 1996 Chevy Suburban 4-wheel drive station wagon configured as a medical first responder – a smaller version of an ambulance, but equipped to pluck skydivers out of trees. Rescue 7 arrived in time to see the Cessna 180 skid sideways to a dusty stop, its propeller dead still.

One of the waiting jumpers ran up to Rescue 7's driver, excitedly pointing toward a white mass of cloth on the ground near the end of the runway.

"It's Alvin! He's hurt! That's him down there," he said. Rescue 7 flipped on its siren and lights and sped down the gravel landing strip to find Alvin Fedoro in the tall grass, eyes closed.

The driver and his medic leaped from Rescue 7 and ran to disconnect the parachute before a stray breeze caught it and dragged their patient away.

Alvin's face was caked in blood. The medic pulled out a disposable airway and was preparing to insert it into the injured man's trachea when a bloody, sputtering cough told him it wouldn't be necessary. He stabilized Alvin's neck and tried to keep him conscious.

"Sir? Can you hear me? Open your eyes if you can hear me."

"Can't open 'em," Alvin groaned. "Too much blood."

The medic staunched the bleeding eyelid enough for Alvin to see what was going on around him. "Talk to me. Stay awake. What day is today, sir?"

"Hurry up with that tourniquet," Alvin said

"What? What did you say? Sir, wake up. Tell me your name."

"Alvin. Name's Alvin. Get a tourniquet on my leg."

"Why do you need a tourniquet, Alvin?"

"Leg... torn off... I'll bleed to death..." he stammered.

The driver returned with the backboard and a cervical collar. While the medic strapped Alvin down, the driver quickly checked the victim's extremities. He had to push the tall grass off to one side in order to see the legs.

"*Good God.*"

"What is it?" the medic asked.

"Not sure." He held up a loose loop of yellow webbing – the static line. "It's fouled tight around the boot. Man, that must've hurt like a bitch." The driver easily untied the strap, and the static line relaxed its grip on Alvin's ankle.

"What's that thing tied to the end of it?"

Alvin heard them talking about his leg as though it were still attached. "My leg... it's still there?"

TeeJay Laarzen was in better shape than the other three jumpers jogging down the length of the runway. He reached Alvin thirty yards ahead of the others and didn't appear to be out of breath.

"How can I help?"

"I think we got it under control," the driver said. "No, wait. What's that thing hooked to the static line?"

"Looks like the pilot's seat. Hey, Alvin. Wake up," TeeJay said.

"I'm awake," he mumbled.

"Looks like you jerked the pilot's seat right out of the plane."

"I did *what*?"

"The static line. It's hooked to the seat."

He struggled to sit up but the medic had already tied him down by the chest and the forehead. "Can't be. I never hook to the seat, not counting today. I'll bet Rudy is pissed."

The driver and medic lifted Alvin onto the wheeled stretcher. He was regaining sensation and the swelling pain in his right knee became intense and happy, reminding him with each throb that the leg was still attached.

"I screwed up," he said, "but it still counts as a jump."

"Is that your thousand, then?" TeeJay asked.

"Am I wearing pants?"

"Yeah."

"Then, no. I still got one more."

Shooter
Two-Two-Five

ONE

Ensign Gary Short stood at attention in the Pensacola morning sun, the last man in the last line of the last formation of his Aviation Officer Candidate class. Eight weeks of marching, inspections, sweating, inspections, lectures, marching, and inspections were finally over. This was Graduation Day.

Two hours earlier, the Candidates had held up their right hands and repeated the oath of office. Now, they stood in ranks, wearing the official khaki of unrestricted line officers in the United States Navy, their armpits already darkening in the early summer swelter.

One more ritual remained, the final inspection by their Drill Instructor, Gunnery Sergeant H. Wilson Meters, USMC. The Gunny stood tall, spoke Truth, tolerated no slur against the Corps, and rained down Hell's fury upon the head and shoulders of any Candidate who dared look him in the eye.

Ensign Short didn't dare. He enjoyed a healthy fear of Marine Gunnery Sergeants, so he stared straight ahead and used his peripheral vision to watch Gunny Meters work his way down through three rows of graduates.

The temperature built rapidly as The Gunny inspected each of the officers in turn. First their shoes, then their belt buckles, buttons, collar devices, haircut, and finally, the metal emblems on their khaki pisscutters.

It was slow, sweaty, and pointless. Even if The Gunny were to find a missing belt loop or a mismatched sock, he couldn't do anything about it.

According to local legend, one class of Candidates had actually stood their final inspection with their flies open and the only thing the DI could do was salute each man and say "Sir" and get paid.

The first time an officer receives a salute, he is supposed to hand over a silver dollar. It's a Navy tradition, old and inviolable. With deliberate slowness, Gunny Meters finished with the first row and marched into the second. One by one, he inspected each new officer, snapped a salute, shook their hand, and took their coin.

Ensign Short was the last officer in the formation. The Gunny was out of view but Short could hear him working his way down the final row. There was nothing to do but wait and try to ignore the heat.

The sun beat down and burned his exposed neck. His cotton uniform shirt had become sticky with perspiration. A random nerve end sparked to life on the inside of his left eyebrow, an itch that refused to be ignored and could not be scratched. Not in formation.

To reach up and dig at the eyebrow with a fingernail would be blissful relief, but nobody else was scratching so Ensign Short kept his arms pinned by his sides. He tried thinking about something else, but the only issues he could concentrate on were the heat and the itching eyebrow.

He tried furrowing his brow, hoping to trap the itch in a wrinkle and, with luck, smother it. Instead, the prickly point squeezed out a single, pinpoint bead of perspiration. It was soon joined by another, and then another, until a full-blown droplet of sweat dangled between Ensign Short's eyebrows, tickling and itching and slowing time.

He could see The Gunny approach and face the officer standing next to him. Short waited impatiently, staring straight ahead. Out of the corner of his eye, he watched Gunny Meters snap a salute and shake hands. He heard a perfunctory "Congratulations, sir" and then The Gunny took the coin and stepped back.

Finally, it was *his* turn! He tightened his grip on the sharp-edged new silver dollar in his left hand.

The Gunny stepped in front of Ensign Short and executed a left face. Less than two feet apart, both men stood at attention, staring at one another. The Gunny's eyes were dull blue, wrinkled and cool as ice. Ensign Short's were wildly blinking from the sweat between his eyes.

A combination of quivering eyebrows, gravity, and the alignment of celestial bodies tugged the droplet free of its moorings and it traveled, hesitantly, down the ridge of his nose to the tip, where it stopped.

The Gunny stared at the glistening nexus, his face betraying neither concern nor amusement. He then cast his gaze downward to inspect the Ensign's shoes.

At that precise instant, the heavy bead of nose sweat pulled loose, arced out and away, and fell freely down, down, and down, ending its karmic journey in a splash on the brightly spit-polished toe of the old Marine's left shoe.

Gunny Meters stopped the inspection and looked up, a barely noticeable tic afflicting his left lower eyelid. He pulled his right hand up to the bill of his cap in a slow, evenly paced salute.

As he took Ensign Short's coin, Gunny Meters smiled. "Exemplary aim, Ensign. You'd make a helluva Snake driver if you was a Marine. Pity."

TWO

Lieutenant Luke "Puke" Harrison's F-14 was VF-114's number one Ready Bird on the Nimitz. Sitting on the deck, shackled to the catapult with both engines turning at idle power, the massive jet would burn through its fuel reserve in fifty-three minutes.

Luke checked his clock and keyed the intercom. "Wake up back there, Jungle." His new Radar Intercept Officer hadn't been asleep. Lieutenant (junior grade) George Jim, call sign "Jungle", had been checking and cross-checking each of the six Phoenix radar-guided missiles they would carry into battle.

"I'm awake, Puke."

"It's ten o'clock. Time for Ivan. You ready for your first dance with a Bear?" The Soviets kept to a tight schedule, as they had for the entire month that the Nimitz battle group had been at sea in the Eastern Mediterranean.

"I can dance, but where's my date?"

Luke was thinking up a witty response when the voice of the Air Boss boomed in their headsets, familiar and urgent. *"Launch the number one Ready bird. CIC is tracking a single inbound."*

Lieutenant Harrison rolled in afterburner, pushed his head back against the ejection seat, saluted the catapult officer and waited. Two long seconds later, he was climbing away from the Nimitz, accelerating through one hundred fifty miles per hour.

He switched his active frequency to talk with Nimitz' Combat Information Center. "CIC, Aardvark One airborne."

"Roger, Aardvark, come left to one one five and climb to angels two fifty. Bogey is three hundred nautical and closing at two nine zero knots."

Thirty seconds after launch, Luke and his RIO were climbing through fifteen thousand feet, wings swept back dart-like, dragging a supersonic shock wave in their wake.

"Right on time." Jungle said on the intercom.

"Make sure the AWG-9 is cold and let's have the notes on this bogey as soon as I pull alongside."

The Russians were coming out of the Black Sea corridor at the same time every day, flying close enough to gather radar signatures for their identification database. They kept their distance and held to a predictable schedule so that nobody got trigger-happy.

The protocol was simple and respected by both sides. Aardvark One would leave their missile radar off and join up on the left wing of the intruder. They'd wave at the pilot, take photographs, and tell the intruder to turn around. In return, the Russians would turn their defensive gun control radar off, point their tail guns up, wave and take pictures.

It only took fifteen minutes to catch the bogey, a Soviet Tupolev Tu-95 "Bear" bomber. Aardvark One passed the Bear head-on with a closing speed of more than a thousand miles per hour.

Luke pulled the power lever back to idle and let air resistance drag his speed down below five hundred. Then he banked the plane into a tight turn, G-forces multiplying the drag until the F-14 had slowed to just under three fifty and was pointed back at the Bear's rear end.

Luke caught up with the Soviet bomber less than a minute later, slowing down to match the Russian's lumbering speed and taking up escort position off their left wingtip.

He had danced this same dance eighteen times before. When the Russians closed to within 250 miles of the fleet they would turn away, their data-gathering mission completed.

Luke switched his radio to the GUARD frequency and transmitted an intercept warning. "Unidentified Soviet aircraft, turn right and leave the area immediately."

The Bear didn't answer. Luke tried again, and again there was no answer. He switched to the Soviet air-to-air frequency, and again the Bear ignored the transmission.

Jungle looked up the tail number of the Bear in their intercept intelligence notebook. *"That's Major Vasily Leonov's bird."*

"Then something is fishy, Jungle. Vasily's a talker. You think their radio is out?"

"Can't tell. Hey, Puke... check out their guns."

Luke looked at the tail cone of the Bear. The two radar-aimed GSh-23 cannon barrels stuck out the back, pointed down. Protocol with the Russians called for the guns to be pointed up, indicating they were on "safe".

Luke keyed his transmitter. "Soviet Tu-95, respond. Vasily, it's Luke Harrison. Talk to me."

Silence, and the Bear was getting closer to the fleet. Clearly, today's rules were different. Luke tried talking to the pilot in Russian. Jungle came on the intercom, laughing. *"Hey, Puke, that was awful."*

But from the Soviet bomber, silence. It was still on its original course, ten miles from the fleet barrier point.

Luke transmitted his situation back to the Nimitz. "CIC, Aardvark One. Bogey is Soviet Tu-95, negative contact. Advise."

Luke pulled closer to the giant bomber's port wing and made hand signals telling the Bear to turn away.

Nimitz crackled over Luke's headset, *"Aardvark One, CIC, bogey is designated Ivan One, possibly hostile, approaching failsafe."*

"CIC, Aardvark has visual on Ivan. Be advised aft guns are port arms."

The F-14's intercom came alive. *"Puke! Ivan's fire control radar just went hot! AWG-9 is still in standby mode. You want I should light up this fucker?"*

"No, wait. Watch his guns."

Luke was right. The Russian pointed his twin cannons up, then down, and again, up and down. Jungle keyed the intercom and said, *"Ivan's cold again. What's with this guy?"*

"Vasily's telling us something's wrong. I'll bet he's got KGB on board. See that face in the aft bubble? Watch this." Luke advanced the throttle and slid the F-14 forward until he was even with the cockpit. "There's Vasily in the left seat, see him?"

"Yeah, so?" Thirty seconds later, a new face appeared in the cockpit window. *"Hey! There's that guy from the aft bubble!"*

"Yeah, now watch this," Luke said. He slid the F-14 back toward the Su-95's tail. A minute later, the same face showed up in the aft bubble.

"Bingo! There he is. That guy's gotta be tired by now."

"Yup. Not much room in that little tunnel. Let's give him a workout," Luke said, pulling forward to the cockpit again. He waved at Vasily, who was clearly laughing at the political officer's plight.

A gloved hand appeared in the pilot's window, the middle finger extended straight up.

"Aardvark One, CIC. Ivan One is past failsafe, now designated Hostile One."

Before Luke could object, the KGB officer appeared in the cockpit. Even from the F-14, Luke could see trouble brewing in the Russian bomber. A second later, the giant plane accelerated to three hundred knots, then three-fifty, then four hundred. Luke added power to compensate and stay on the Bear's wing.

"Aardvark One, CIC. Hostile One at line of engagement. Break off and make weapons hot."

"Did you copy, Jungle?"

"Roger, weapons hot."

The flight officer brought the Tomcat's AWG-9 fire control radar to full power and selected one of the Phoenix air-to-air missiles.

"Hold off a sec. This is a KGB game. It's a feint."

Luke hailed the Nimitz. "CIC, Aardvark One. Hostile One is NORDO – no transmissions at all. I believe there's a KBG on board. Guys, he's making a political point, not an attack. Copy?"

"Aardvark One, CIC, Hostile One is inside the line. You are cleared to engage."

Luke couldn't believe the order. Shooting down a Soviet bomber was a bad way to start the day.

"CIC, Aardvark One, say again your last."

"Aardvark One, CIC, break off escort and engage Hostile One.."

Jungle's voice popped through the static. *"OK, Puke. AWG is hot and tied into Phoenix number one."*

"Dammit, Jungle! Freeze the weapons and hang on. He's not hostile. They got a pushy KGB officer on board, that's all."

"We're cleared to engage, Puke."

"That's what we're gonna do. I'm just not in the mood to kill people today."

Luke pushed the F-14's twin power levers forward into afterburner. He rushed ahead of the Bear and pulled his nose up into a giant, lazy loop. Over the top, he held power steady and popped through the sound barrier, letting gravity pull him faster through mach 1.2, then 1.5, pulling back on the stick as he reached the bottom of the loop moving at almost twice the speed of sound.

Aardvark One leveled off two miles behind the Bear and five hundred feet below it. The bomber was still on course toward the fleet.

Jungle's voice boomed on the intercom. *"Ivan's gun radar just went active. ECM deployed."*

Luke closed on the bomber in a matter of seconds, the Tomcat's Electronic Countermeasures package blinding the Bear's guns. The F-14 passed directly beneath the big plane but over eight hundred miles knots faster.

"Hang on back there."

"Puke, this is a bad idea," Jungle warned.

Luke abruptly pulled up and shot vertically in front of the Bear, leaving behind a pair of side-by-side supersonic tornados. The maneuver is known as "thumping".

The Russian flew into the spinning wake a quick second later. "Fire" and "Master Caution" lights flared on the bomber's panel. Two of the Bear's engines flamed out instantly. The flight engineer was thrown clear of his seat and fractured his arm on the edge of his fold out worktable. One "auxiliary crewmember" was knocked unconscious.

The wounded Bear immediately turned and limped toward home. The Soviet Air Division commander filed a diplomatic protest with the White House, which responded by faxing a photograph of a gloved Russian hand making an obscene gesture. The Russian pilot was disciplined severely.

Lieutenant Harrison was transferred to the VT-6 "Shooters" for duty as a primary flight instructor. He would never again see the inside of a jet cockpit. Everybody knew he was coming and they knew his new job was punishment.

Sensitive to the needs of their newcomer and wanting to avoid dredging up painful memories of better days, they retired his old call sign and had a flight suit embroidered with his new nickname. Luke had no trouble finding his squadron locker. His new call sign was neatly painted on the door.

"THUMPER".

THREE

"*Thumper*? Is there a *Thumper* in here?"

There were only five people in the VT-6 Ready Room, but Ensign Short's question went unanswered. He felt foolish calling out a nickname but that's all the Schedules desk had given him.

Short looked around the room. Two men in flight suits were sitting at a small side table looking over a map. Two enlisted men were working behind the Operations counter. One officer sat alone, dressed in a flight suit, drinking coffee and mashing small handfuls of popcorn into his mouth.

Short walked up behind him and cleared his throat. The older pilot needed a shave. His flight suit was stained and unzipped, making it easy to see that the pilot needed to wear a t-shirt. "THUMPER" was neatly embroidered above the left breast pocket.

"Are you Thumper?" Short asked.

"Budweiser," the pilot answered, not looking up.

"Your flight suit says *Thumper*."

"No, you owe me a beer. I like Bud."

"Why do I owe you a beer?"

"'Cause you asked a stupid question."

"I only wanted to know if you were Thumper."

"What does it say on my flight suit?"

"*Thumper*."

"Does it not stand to reason, therefore, that I might prob'ly be this Thumper guy you're yellin' for?"

Ensign Short's face reddened. "Sorry."

"Sorry won't do. Beer fixes dumb. What d'ya want?"

"Pardon?"

"Shit. You're my FAM-Oh, aren't you? Siddown. You got any flight time?"

Short shook his head. "Never flown anything."

"Well, well. My lucky day. That's two more Buds at the "O" Club tonight. One for bustin' your airplane cherry and one for takin' you sight-seein'."

"Sight seeing?"

"Didn't they tell you? FAM-Zero is a freebie. We're just going up to help you get oriented. You can't fail FAM-Oh."

Thumper tossed the remnants of his coffee and popcorn into the trash. For the next half hour, he reviewed emergency procedures, weight and balance, and basic flight controls with Ensign Short. Thumper fished around blindly in his leather case and pulled out a badly folded sectional map of their flight area.

"Sorry 'bout the messy map. It's the one I always use for FAM-Oh's." He pointed at a rough circle drawn over and over in blue ink. "This here is Whiting," he said. Then he pointed out other airfields they'd visit today, tracing a line with his finger from the messy blue circle to another one just like it. In the middle of the ring was the tiny Alabama town of Brewton. Farther north, the Evergreen airport was marked the same way.

"Evergreen's got a great snack bar. Maybe we'll stop off there for lunch. C'mon. Time to fly."

They stopped at the maintenance hangar first. Thumper spent a few minutes flipping through a metal binder full of logs and gripes for their assigned plane. The cover of the binder had "2-2-5" stenciled neatly in the center.

He initialed the top sheet and handed the book back. "Let's go," he said. "Two-two-five is on the first row." The two men walked out of the hangar into the bright sunlight, squinting.

They walked down a long row of nearly identical T-34's. A few of the planes had snazzy-looking shark's teeth painted on their cowlings. "What's with the teeth?" Short asked.

"Those are pranged birds," Thumper said. "Some shrink told the front office to paint teeth on damaged planes so pilots would quit grounding 'em for no good reason."

"Well, did it work?"

"Better than they figured. Now it's the *new* ones nobody wants to fly." They walked up to their assigned plane, the number "225" painted on its side. There were no shark's teeth on this one.

Short appeared quick-witted and eager. He showed no reluctance to get his hands dirty as he explored every access door, hatch and cover, asking questions throughout the fifteen-minute preflight.

Both pilots climbed onto the port wing and slid the canopy open. Ensign Short squirmed into the front cockpit and belted himself in, parachute straps first, followed by a four-point restraint system that looked like it came out of a stock car.

"None of these straps are particularly snug," he said.

"Don't worry. There's never been a successful bailout from a T-34C."

"That's comforting."

Thumper climbed into the back seat and strapped himself in. He plugged his headset into the radio/intercom and clicked the intercom switch.

Short's headset came alive with a click and static from the instructor's seat. Thumper's voice cut through the noise.

"Hey, Ensign... you gonna barf when we get up there?"

Short pressed the Mike button and transmitted, "I can try."

A different voice came across the headset. *"Aircraft calling Whiting Ground, say again your last."*

"Push down for intercom, up for radio," Thumper said.

"Sorry."

"Budweiser forgives all sins. That's four. You're a fun date, Ensign."

"Aircraft calling Whiting Ground, say again your last."
"OK, Short. Light the fires."
"Me?"
"I couldn't tell... was that a dumb question?"
Short reconsidered asking again. He checked the storage pocket and pulled out the NATOPS checklist. "Prop clear...CLEAR!" he shouted, leaning out so any stray candidates or dogs would know to get out from under the nose of the plane.

"Starter switch on...ten volts, ignition light OK, fuel pressure light off, oil pressure...*up!*" The prop started turning, the electric motor spinning the engine gradually faster, the "click-click-click" of the engine's automatic igniters audible over the static in Short's helmet. He kept his left hand on the condition lever and his eyes on the turbine tach.

"Twelve percent...feathering..." he pushed the lever forward, introducing fuel into the compressed air inside the PT-6A engine. The fuel caught fire, and the hot gases pushed the little turboprop engine faster and faster. "ITT normal...sixty percent," he announced, cutting the starter switch off as the plane's propeller spun alive, slicing at the air.

Normally, the instructor would have had to do the entire engine start procedure. *"You did OK on the start. I have the plane,"* Thumper said over the intercom. *"Let's taxi out."*

He called Whiting Ground Control for clearance to the active runway. *"North Whiting Ground, Shooter Two-Two-Five rolling for the active with India, VFR local to the North."*

The control answered with a machine-gun transmission, *"Shooter Two-Two-Five is cleared to the active, number one hold short, contact north tower on one-two-one point four. G'day sir."*

"Two-Two-Five," he answered, switching to the tower frequency for takeoff clearance. *"North tower, Shooter Two-Two-Five ready."*

"Two-Two-Five, North tower, cleared for takeoff, left turn when able to three-six-oh, maintain two thousand."

Thumper handled the takeoff and climbout, setting a course roughly north, keeping the main road off his right wing. That would take him directly to Brewton and its outlying landing field.

They flew over the little Alabama town low enough to get a good view of the runways but well above the traffic pattern. A few red and white T-34's were visible below, practicing landings.

They pressed on northward. A few minutes later, I-65 was visible through the haze, a thin ribbon of white concrete marking the southern border of their practice area. Short was intrigued by the way things looked when seen from up high but he wasn't there just to be a passenger.

"Ensign, take the controls. Hold this course and altitude."

Ensign Short had little trouble pointing the nose of the plane where he wanted it to go but it was more difficult to maintain a constant altitude. One second he was at 2000 feet, he looked away, then when he looked back again he was at 2250.

"OK, let's climb to three thousand and I'll go through some basic flyin' stuff. I have the controls."

Thumper demonstrated how to coordinate turns with rudder, how to climb, how to descend. Short paid attention and copied the maneuvers well. He was more proficient at controlling his altitude but it still wasn't easy. The afternoon air had become turbulent and the instrument needles were bouncing everywhere.

Thumper wasn't making his workload any easier. *"Is your visor down?"* his voice crackled over the intercom. As soon as Short reached up to pull the visor latch on his helmet, Thumper asked, *"What's our altitude supposed to be?"*

He searched the instrument panel and discovered he couldn't fly the plane, watch the airspeed and find the altimeter at the same time. There, the altimeter...oh, NO! It was showing nearly 3500 feet! He had busted his altitude. He pushed the stick forward and eased off on the power control lever.

"*Watch your airspeed, Ensign,*" Thumper admonished, then told him, "*Follow I-65 for another coupla minutes and turn south.*"

Altitude…3300 and descending. Airspeed…180 knots and increasing. Where the hell was the highway? It should've been on the left…no, there it was on the right.

"*OK, Ensign, turn left and head south. And lower your visor when you get a chance…it's NATOPS, son – you gotta do it.*"

Ensign Short could only concentrate on the first part. Where's the CDI? Never mind, just turn a little to the left.

"*What altitude are you looking for, Ensign?*"

Altitude? Altitude…2200! Damn! How did THAT happen? Airspeed…200?! Pull back a little…

"*Is your visor down? I'm not asking again,*" Thumper warned. He wasn't really looking at Short's helmet. It was just standard instructor tactics to give the student more than they could handle. He leaned forward a little to dial in the Unicom radio frequency at Brewton. Ensign Short let go of the power lever and reached up one more time to twist the knob that would lower his helmet visor.

The world exploded.

FOUR

Thumper heard a loud POP and noticed the radio panel had turned red and blurry and he couldn't see the numbers any more. He had the strangest feeling he was waking up from a nap, except for the noise.

There was pain in his face. Instinctively, he tried to rub his right eye and found something in the way. Something was stuck there. It didn't hurt, so he pulled on it. A tiny sliver of plastic no more than an inch long slid out from its hiding place in the flesh above his right cheekbone. It was colored dark red.

In fact, everything was dark red and blurry. A storm was blowing wind in through the door. *"Honey! Close the damn door!"* he heard his wife shouting. The front door wanted to stay open all the time and now it...

No. Something's wrong. Storms aren't red.

Thumper looked around. This wasn't his living room... it was the cockpit of a T-34, but he had never seen an airplane like this one. It was painted dark red everywhere and there was no windshield up front.

He shook his head but his vision wouldn't clear. The wind was terrible! It had to be over a hundred miles an hour, whipping everything in the cockpit. He tucked his head to protect his eyes and saw his kneeboard was gone. Thumper looked around the edges of his seat for his kneeboard when he noticed something else missing.

Ensign Short was no longer up front. Where in hell had the student gone? He was just there, dammit!

Thumper flipped his intercom switch and shouted over the wind, "Short! Ensign Short!" No answer. He called him again, and then again, but got nothing but silence in return.

He wiped his finger along the cockpit rail. It came back wet and dark and gooey. There were tiny chunks of bone mixed in with the gore. Thumper swallowed hard. So much damage, so much blood. He felt sick. Something had hit them. Another plane, maybe. Whatever it was, it had taken the student's head completely off.

"*Fly!*" a voice inside his head told him. "*Fly the plane!*"

Thumper had trouble focusing on the instruments. The altimeter showed told him the T-34 was a little below 3000 feet and slowly climbing. The airspeed indicator was smeared in blood and the needle was hard to see, but he had been flying long enough to recognize a wounded engine when he heard one.

He tried to move the stick, but met strong resistance. Rudder pedals seemed to be stuck, too. Control was not going to be possible. There was only enough time to save his life. Thumper tried to remember the bailout procedures but the pain in his eye demanded too much concentration.

He pulled the plugs connecting his helmet to the radio system and unlocked the four-point restraint holding him to his seat. Then he pulled the canopy emergency handle.

A small bottle of CO_2 pushed the rear canopy as far back as it would go. The wind was blowing in a straight line now, no longer swirling. As he turned in his seat to pull himself free, Thumper realized nobody on the ground knew what had happened. A bailout would probably land him in the wilds of the Florida panhandle. He was going to need Search and Rescue to come get him.

He hurriedly switched the radio to the GUARD channel and hit the transmit button "Mayday! Mayday! Mayday! Shooter Two-Two-Five on GUARD. Midair at three thousand feet near Evergreen! Student is dead. Bailing out."

He hadn't noticed the dangling communications plugs. Thumper climbed over the edge of the cockpit and was tugged free as the slipstream sucked him out into the empty air.

He saw the plane falling up away from him and lost precious seconds trying to understand the noise, falling faster, shooting toward the ground at over a hundred miles an hour.

Thumper looked down and saw the ripcord handle on his chest, grabbed it in a panic and yanked it with every ounce of strength he could generate. A very slow half-second passed before the falling stopped. His parachute opened explosively, jerking him backwards in midair and leaving him hanging in the harness with a sore neck.

Everything was suddenly calm and quiet. In the distance, he could hear the doomed T-34C heading south, a dead man at the controls.

FIVE

Out of the blackness of a painful, dreamless sleep, Ensign Short forced his eyes to open. He was slumped in his harness, bent double, head-down below the back of the seat. His legs were soaked darkly in the ooze dripping from that black thing on his lap.

He tried to get a better look at the black thing but it was too close to his face and he couldn't turn his head. A wall of agony stabbed him across the neck and down his right arm. The pain made him tired and sleepy. All he wanted to do was close his eyes and dream.

There was wind coming from somewhere, slapping at his helmet and shaking his head back and forth. He wanted to sleep but the broken collarbone kept waking him up, slipping sharp needles of bone into his flesh from the inside.

Drifting on the edge of awareness, Short wondered at the noise and the wind. Where was he? He forced his memory to work, one problem at a time. Gauges. Levers. Lights.

There was something he had to do… something he wanted to tell Thumper. Slowly, he remembered a dot in the sky, hovering just above the horizon, growing larger.

He was going to ask Thumper about the dot but he was so darn busy just making the altimeter behave, and Thumper kept saying something about his visor. He had to lock his visor.

Had he done it? He couldn't remember. The speck had grown larger and taken shape. It had wings.

Wings!

Ensign Short's memory returned with a frantic urgency. He remembered locking his visor down. He remembered flying the airplane. He remembered the bird – that huge turkey buzzard – and the sound it made as it burst through the Plexiglas windscreen.

There was nothing after that, only the here and now, the pain and the black thing on his lap.

Short forced himself to sit up. The wind whistled at his face through the missing half of the helmet's shattered visor, pushing streamlets of blood from his broken nose around both sides of his face.

He looked at his legs and recognized the black thing. It was the battered lower half of a buzzard, torn in two when it passed through the propeller. Entrails and bone chips and bird blood had exploded in front of him, coating the interior of the T-34 with a reddish-black tinge.

He reached for the carcass with his right hand and was stopped rudely by his fractured collarbone. Switching to his left hand, he pried the dead bird from his lap and heaved it over his shoulder. The wind carried it back into Thumper's seat.

"Sorry, Thumper!" Short shouted on the intercom. Getting no answer, he twisted in his seat to try and see whether the instructor was hurt. The pain shooting from his shoulder made him stop twisting and he sat back down, hard.

He tried the intercom again. "Thumper?"

No answer. Maybe the wind noise was too loud. He tried again, shouting into the mike this time, "THUMPER!"

No answer. The pain stabbing him in the neck and shoulder was dizzying. He was sleepy again, but pure instinct told him to stay awake... *awake* damn it! "*What next? What do I do next?*" he asked himself.

Ensign Short tried to recall what little he had been able to see when he turned around. It was no use. All he could remember was the stabbing pain. He wanted to convince himself there could be another way – ANY other way to see behind him and find out how Thumper was doing. There wasn't, though. He'd have to try turning around again.

"*This is gonna really hurt*," he told himself. Then he pushed with both feet and twisted his head at the same time. Clearly, he had vividly underestimated how *much* it would hurt.

Blinded by agony, he fell back into his seat having seen nothing. If Thumper was back there, he wasn't able to fly the plane any more.

"*Bail out*," Short told himself. "*Just bail out.*" It was a good idea. He was injured. His instructor was probably dead. Nobody was flying the plane. The regulations were clear – if the airplane is out of control below 5,000 feet, *bail out*.

He couldn't. He was injured. His instructor might still be alive. And technically, the plane was still under the control of a pilot – even if he was just a student pilot.

The engine sounded like it was working too hard. Short realized that the nose of the airplane was pointed too high. Pretty soon the plane would stop flying altogether.

He pushed the power lever forward just enough to buy a little time and then let go and moved his left hand onto the stick. It felt clumsy and alien but the right arm wouldn't move at all, so the left side would have to do double duty.

He pressed the stick forward to get the nose down. His left hand didn't obey as nicely as the right hand would have. The plane floundered, but after some experimentation the results were good enough. He moved his hand back to the power quadrant, took a deep breath and considered his next move.

He scanned the panel. The hands on the altimeter were still visible even though the glass face was heavily spattered with bird innards. It showed a slow climb, which he figured was better than a fast descent. The radio panel showed the GUARD frequency. That was lucky. Ensign Short keyed the "transmit" button.

"Help. Somebody out there, help me."

SIX

Simultaneously, every military tower, aircraft, and runway duty officer within a radius of ninety miles heard the strange transmission. Pensacola Approach Control was the first to answer.

"Aircraft transmitting on GUARD, Pensacola Approach, say again please."

Ensign Short heard something through his headset, but he couldn't make it out through the deafening wind whipping his face. All he heard clearly was the one word, *"GUARD"*. He felt totally lost, couldn't hear his radio, and couldn't remember the right words to use to let people on the ground know what was going on.

Off to his left he saw the outline of an airfield. Based on its position relative to the city, he guessed he must be near Brewton. Short turned east to fly over the top of the field.

He pulled power back a little and slowed down. His altimeter started moving again, this time losing altitude. He pulled back on the stick to stop the descent, slowing down even faster.

Short juggled the power and stick until he had slowed to a little more than 100 knots. It was tricky, doing everything with one hand.

The field was much closer now. Three runways set in he shape of a triangle... yes, that was Brewton Field.

The wind blasting in through the hole in the Plexiglas was much less painful at the slower speed. His headset crackled with new voices.

"Aircraft on GUARD, Pensacola Approach, say again."

Ensign Short figured they were talking to him. He thumbed the transmit button again, eager to talk to someone who knew more than he did.

"This is Ensign Gary Short. I'm a student Naval Aviator. I'm in trouble and I need a little help." In his excitement, he nearly forgot to identify the plane. "And, ahh… this is Shooter Two-Two-Five."

SEVEN

Lieutenant Ashton "Dago" Cardigo was sitting in the RDO hut next to runway 24 at Brewton. "Runway Duty Officer" was a boring, thankless job, but at least the little wooden hut had windows. In fact, it was nothing BUT windows, all the way around.

Dago was an instructor with the VT-2 "Blackbirds", but today was a duty day. For the next three...no (he looked at his watch) two and a half hours he would sit out in the sun and make sure every plane lowered their landing gear before touching down. They'd do a touch and go and then return to the landing pattern for another try.

Dago used binoculars to visually check each plane just prior to landing, when they called "Gear down and locked." His radio was permanently tuned to the published common UNICOM frequency. He had a second handheld radio in the RDO hut, tuned to 243.0 megahertz – the GUARD frequency.

The first time he heard the call for help, he thought it was one of his students. Dago grabbed his binoculars and scanned the pattern, counting airplanes. One...two...three...four! All of his were accounted for. So who was the joker?

The radio crackled. *"Aircraft on GUARD, Pensacola Approach ...squawk IDENT."*

Silence.

"Aircraft on GUARD, Pensacola Approach ..."

More silence.

"Aircraft on GUARD, Pensacola Approach Control..."

"...dammit! Can't talk now!"

It was the voice Dago had heard earlier. This was more interesting than RDO work.

"Any time, sir, Pensacola Approach on GUARD..."

His emergency radio was silent for several dozen heartbeats. Then that voice again, *"Pensacola, this is Ensign Short on GUARD. Can you hear me?"*

"Affirmative, sir. Are you declaring an emergency?"

"Wait," Ensign Short said. More silence. More empty seconds. Then a crackling transmission, *"...Shooter Two-Two-Five. Mayday."*

"Roger Shooter Two-Two-Five.   Sir, what is your emergency?"

The voice sounded high-pitched and strained. *"My instructor's hurt. I've hit some kind of a bird. Hey, guys, I'm getting close to Brewton. Can you help me get down, please?"*

Dago opened the door of the RDO hut with his foot and stumbled out into the open sunlight, nearly dropping his binoculars. He scanned the sky in every direction, counting out loud. His own squadron's group of four were still in the pattern, but nobody else...

There! A tiny dot west of the field. He raised his binoculars and tried to hold them steady. The dot was a little less dot-like through the glasses, just enough...Yes! It was a T-34! Much too high for the pattern, it had to be Two-Two-Five.

Dago jumped back into the RDO hut and waited for the first lull in transmissions.

"...Two-Five, can you squawk seven-seven-zero-zero and IDENT, please."

"Negative, Pensacola. I can't move my right arm."

Dago interrupted, "Pensacola Approach, Brewton RDO. I have Two-Two-Five in sight."

"Brewton RDO, Pensacola. Are you LSO-qualified, sir?"

"Pensacola, that's affirmative. What's the plan?" They wouldn't have asked about whether he was a Landing Safety

Officer unless they were going to saddle him with this situation.

A different voice came on GUARD. *"Pensacola Approach, Whiting tower...request handoff. He's one of ours. SAR bird is airborne. Can you keep all traffic clear of Brewton?"*

"Whiting, Pensacola...affirmative, sir."

The voice sounded familiar, but it was definitely not the controller. *"Brewton, Whiting. Dago, this is Paul Meeks. We've got us a full dance card."*

Commander Meeks was the skipper of VT-6. Dago had flown with him during Instructor Pilot school.

"Whiting, Brewton RDO. What can I do, skipper?"

Meeks filled the RDO in. *"We've activated SAR, but right now they're busy trying to find a survivor. I need you take over as LSO. Sorry 'bout this, Dago...Two-Two-Five is all yours."*

"Whiting, Brewton... the student reported that the instructor was in the plane."

"I don't know. We're responding to a civilian report of a chute near Evergreen."

"I have to assume both crew are still in 225. I can bring 'em in the active."

"Negative Dago. Not your call. The kid is FAM-0. Keep it simple. Get him under a chute as quick as you can."

"Skipper, the IP may be alive."

"Don't make me repeat the order, Dago. Get that student under a parachute. Copy?"

It took a few seconds for this order to sink in. Somebody was going to die today and the LSO was going to get the blame.

"Dago. Do you copy?"

"Yes, sir. Affirmative."

EIGHT

"Shooter Two-Two-Five, Brewton on GUARD, how do you hear?" Dago called.

"*I hear you OK,*" Short answered.

"Did they tell me right? This is your FAM-zero?"

"*Affirmative, sir.*"

"Can you tell me your altitude and airspeed?"

"*Uhh, thirty-three hundred and about a hundred knots, sir.*"

Dago liked those numbers. A bailout should be easy, and the prevailing wind would drift the pilot right onto the airfield. "Two-Two-Five, Brewton. Turn left to two seven zero and pull out your NATOPS. We'll go through the emergency egress steps together."

"*Negative, Brewton,*" Short objected. "*I'm hurt and the instructor is out cold. Bailout is not an option.*"

"Bailout is your only option, Ensign. Come left to two seven zero."

"*Negative, Brewton. I'll try to land.*"

Dago let this idea sink in. The T-34 was relatively easy to fly, if you knew what you were doing. But landings in any kind of plane were tricky. He wondered whether this student had enough experience.

"How many hours do you have?"

"*Almost one.*"

Dago laughed, "No, not in the T-34. Total hours."

"*I told you. This is my first flight.*"

"Are you shitting me? Christ! Stand by." He leaned against the LSO shack and tapped the microphone against his forehead. His patience ran out quickly. "Ensign Short, I'm ordering you to bail out. That's an order."

"Negative, sir. Two-Two-Five declines."

"Are you refusing a lawful order, Mister Short? I'm a Lieutenant, you know. I outrank you."

"Affirmative, sir. I guess this means I'm in trouble."

"Two-Two-Five. If you don't bail out you'll crash that plane. You'll get killed."

"Maybe not. But I won't leave Thumper."

"Two-Two-Five, did you say Thumper's your IP?"

"Affirmative, sir."

"Stand by, Two-Two-Five."

Dago picked up the mike to his UNICOM radio. He needed to get his students out of the traffic pattern.

"All aircraft in vicinity of Brewton, the field is closed...repeat, Brewton Field is closed. All Blackbird aircraft in the pattern at Brewton, this is the RDO. Wave off and return to base. Wave off and return to base. Exit the pattern to the south, climb to one thousand feet and contact Whiting tower on button FOUR."

Now to buy a little time for Ensign Short.

"Shooter Two-Two-Five, Brewton RDO on GUARD... maintain altitude and start turning slowly to the left. Can you do that?"

"Affirmative, Brewton."

Dago stepped outside and scanned the traffic pattern. His four planes had already turned south, heading home. He picked up his binoculars and located Two-Two-Five again.

All of a sudden, he was very lonely. He was disobeying Paul Meeks' orders and would have to pay the price later. *Bad time for feelin' sorry for yourself*, he thought. Dago pushed his emotions out of the way. It was time to concentrate on the student.

"Two-Two-Five, Brewton on GUARD…Mister Short, how badly are you hurt?"

"I don't really know, pretty bad, I guess. Something in my neck or shoulder is broke, so I can't move my right arm. I got a Master Caution light but I got no windshield, so it's kinda hard to see. Think I broke my nose, too…it's all bloody."

"Two-Two-Five, watch your turn. Straighten out on a heading of zero nine zero. Maintain airspeed between one hundred and one two zero knots. Do you understand?"

"Negative, Brewton. It's mighty loud up here. Do what again?"

Dago spoke more slowly, "Two-Two-Five, stop turning and fly straight."

"Roger, Brewton."

"I'm going to bring you in onto runway two-four, Shortie. It's the longest." It also pointed away from the city of Brewton. Just in case.

NINE

The wind blasting through Two-Two-Five forced spasms of tears to flood Short's eyes, but through the haze he could see the nose pointing back toward Brewton field. He leveled the wings and called the RDO.

"Brewton, Two-Two-Five, turn complete. What's next, sir?"

"Two-Two-Five, look down to your left. Can you make out the runway that points along your course?"

"I see it. The number twenty-four is painted on the end. I'm almost parallel."

"OK, Two-Two-Five, we need to bleed off some altitude. Pull back the power control lever just a little bit."

Short edged the lever backwards, listening to the engine as it relaxed. Almost immediately, his vertical speed indicator needle pointed down, settling roughly halfway between zero and negative one.

"Two-Two-Five, what's your rate of descent?"

"Brewton, Two-Two-Five is showing about five hundred feet a minute."

"Good job, Shortie. Now remember how far you pulled the lever, and try to move it back where it started."

Ensign Short moved the lever forward a quarter of an inch, heard the PT-6A respond, and watched as the VSI crept back toward zero.

"Brewton, got it...Two-Two-Five's got it. I'm leveled off, now."

"OK, Shortie, that's how you're going to control your descent. Now let's bleed off some altitude. Pull the power back just like before."

Ensign Short gently reduced power a quarter inch. The engine slowed. The VSI showed a slight descent, again.

"Brewton, Two-Two-Five is descending."

"Roger that, Shortie. Watch your altimeter. What's it showing now?"

"Brewton, Two-Two-Five…is, uh, twenty-eight hundred, sir."

"That's good. Hold it there for a couple of minutes. We'll level off again at two thousand feet."

"Brewton, Two-Two-Five… I'm past the airfield. It's behind me now."

"Roger Two-Two-Five …roger that. We'll turn around in a little bit. Standby for my instructions."

Brewton Municipal slid by under his wing. Far below, Ensign Short could see trucks moving into position near the approach end of runway 24. Fire trucks. He hadn't considered it until now, but there was a chance he might survive the upcoming crash.

He hated the thought of living through the landing just to burn to death.

TEN

Dago kept an eye on his watch. Ninety seconds ticked by. He checked the position of Two-Two-Five, heading away slowly.

"Shooter Two-Two-Five, Brewton …what's your altitude now, Shortie?"

A brief silence, then the radio hissed, *"Nineteen hundred feet. Want power?"*

"Affirmative. Add a little power."

Ten seconds passed. *"Brewton, Two-Two-Five is level at eighteen hundred feet."*

"Good job, Two-Two-Five. Now hold your heading for another minute or so."

"OK."

Ensign Short sounded tired and frustrated. Dago dismissed the thought. He had to figure out how to teach somebody with only one hand how to fly and how to land on their first attempt, without killing anybody.

He had one thing in common with Ensign Short. Neither of them had done anything like this before.

"Two-Two-Five, Brewton…let's get the gear down. On the left, in front of the power lever, the knob that looks like a wheel. Pull it toward you and push it down."

"Roger."

It took several seconds for the wheels to drop down and lock, but Dago could see them come out through his binoculars. Hanging out in the wind, they would slow the T-34 and make it start descending. Dago had anticipated the extra drag.

"Shortie, add a little power to keep your speed up. Call me when you're stabilized."

He waited for Ensign Short to experiment with the power setting. Only a little extra thrust would be required, but with a beginner at the controls it might take quite a while to get the plane back into balance. It took nearly thirty seconds.

"Brewton, Two-Two-Five is level. Altitude sixteen hundred. Airspeed...'bout one-ten."

"OK, Shortie. Now it gets a little busy. Here's the plan..." Dago took a deep breath, hoping he could pull this off. "In a minute, you're gonna make a left turn and line up on the runway the best you can. I'll call for power cuts now and then and guide you down. Got me so far?"

"Brewton...yes, sir."

"When you're over the runway, I'll tell you to cut power. When I do that, you pull the power lever all the way back and let the plane land itself. Then get on the brakes and keep the nose pointed down the runway. Got it?"

"Yes, sir."

"Two-Two-Five, Brewton...here we go. Good luck. Do not make any further transmissions. Turn your landing lights on...two toggle switches under the gear knob..."

"Got 'em."

"Stay off the radio and just listen. You're gonna have enough to do."

ELEVEN

Ensign Short caught himself before acknowledging the last order.   Instead, he reached forward with his left hand and flicked both landing lights on.   Then he strained to hear above the wind noise.

"Two-Two-Five, Brewton...turn left and line up with runway two-four."

He pressed the stick to the left and touched the rudder on the same side, keeping the T-34 in balance.   The turn was painfully slow and at the same time, frighteningly fast.   It took nearly a minute to turn completely around.   Short watched Brewton Municipal ease into view from the left.   He grinned when he saw runway 24, right in front of his nose.   Pure luck, but he'd take it.   He rolled out of the turn.

The radio came alive again.   *"Two-Two-Five...reduce power like you did before."*

He pulled power back a half inch or so, but the plane responded by pitching the nose sharply down!

Startled, Short let go of the power lever and grabbed the stick.   A little back pressure and the plane's nose pitched back up to where it had started.

Something was wrong.   This just didn't feel right.   The plane was mushy and unresponsive.   He looked at the airspeed indicator.   The needle was moving counter clockwise, passing through eighty knots.   Adrenaline poured into his brain.

Speed! He needed speed, *now*!

Short lightened up his grip on the stick, allowing it to come forward a little. The altimeter slowly unwound as his airspeed increased. When it hit one hundred knots, he quickly moved his left hand over to the elevator trim wheel. He rolled it back slightly, felt the nose of the plane respond, and watched the airspeed indicator settle near one hundred and five.

"Ooh," he grunted in relief, looked up and discovered he had drifted to the right of the runway centerline.

"Shortie, you're a little high, take off a little bit of power."

Ensign Short tapped the power control lever with his middle finger, moving it back a tiny amount. The engine eased and Two-Two-Five started down, toward the near end of the runway and the giant number "24". Everything was getting closer and bigger by the second.

He tapped a little rudder to keep his plane lined up with the runway. The altimeter showed 850 feet. Short told himself to forget the damn altimeter. Just do what the RDO said to do. That runway sure looked close.

"Two-Two-Five, looking good so far...I'm gonna put you down halfway down the runway...rate of descent looks good..."

Short kept his hand on the stick and looked at the VSI. The needle was bouncing up and down as the T-34 hit the thermals boiling off the end of the runway. His right wing answered one of these bumps, pushing Two-Two-Five into a left bank. Ensign Short fought back, shoving the stick to the right. The plane fishtailed, yawing to the left.

"Don't fight the turbulence. Forget the stick... just point the nose straight with the rudder pedals."

It didn't sound right, but Short tapped the rudder. Two-Two-Five responded snappily, leveling its wings. Still a half mile from the end of the runway, Short saw wasn't going to make it.

"Add a little power..."

He pushed the power lever up a quarter of an inch. The nose tipped up toward the horizon, stopping the descent. As the nose lifted, the extra power put the plane into a slow roll to the left, drifting away from the runway centerline. Dago saw it happening and radioed for Short to make a correction.

"Right rudder, right rudder..."

He pushed on the right rudder pedal a little bit, then a little more until the roll stopped and reversed direction. Wings level, Two-Two-Five was once again pointed down the center of runway 24.

"OK, Shortie... rudder and power, rudder and power... don't go much lower ..."

It was all Short could do to keep the nose pointed down the runway. A quarter mile from the approach end of 24, Two-Two-Five was in a slight climb. Winds were light, but a crosswind had pushed the plane to the left of the runway. Short concentrated on getting back over the centerline. Airspeed would just have to take care of itself.

Over the end of the runway, Ensign Short fought the crosswind with more right rudder. The plane yawed right and started a slow roll, left wing high. He relaxed his right leg and allowed the plane to roll left on its own. He had no idea how fast he was going. He was too busy fighting an invisible undertow trying to drag him away from the centerline.

"Shortie...cut HALF your power ..."

Ensign Short pulled the power lever back about an inch. The drift stopped suddenly, but the right rudder was still pushed in. The T-34 started rolling to the right as the airspeed bled away, fifty feet over the runway!

He pushed the left rudder and caught the roll, but watched helplessly as his airplane slowed and wallowed toward the ground. Twenty feet above the runway, he last thing he did was look at his airspeed indicator.

He was going seventy knots, too slow to fly. The rudders started shivering beneath his feet, then shaking, hammering at his legs. He heard the RDO say something on the radio. Then the plane quit flying and dropped onto the runway.

Short felt the broken collarbone stab at him one last time.

TWELVE

Two-Two-Five flew over the RDO hut, looking almost normal except for the open canopy and an empty back seat. The engine sounded wrong, somehow. Weak.

"Shortie…add a little power, *add power*," Dago ordered, but it was already too late.

From behind, the landing approach looked almost normal. But the plane was flying too slow and was drifting into a lazy yaw, wallowing on the edge of a stall and losing precious height.

Two-Two-Five finally surrendered and stopped flying, fifty feet above the runway. One wing dipped, then the other, then the little plane fluttered and dropped, slamming flat against the asphalt wheels first, bouncing and skipping to the left.

Dago keyed his mike. "Shortie, cut power and hit the brakes. Hit the brakes!"

In the distance, smoke billowed from the T-34's wheels as it skidded sideways, its brakes locked. Brewton's fire trucks converged from both sides and sprayed purple-K powder into the engine intake, forcing the turboprop motor to flame out and stop. The sound of the propellers winding down made Dago smile.

"Whiting Field, Brewton RDO on GUARD. Two-Two-Five is on the deck. Be advised, runway two-four at Brewton is closed."

THIRTEEN

The impact of the plane's belly flop jerked Short's right arm down, pulling apart the ends of his broken collarbone and then letting them slam back together. He remembered screaming, dizzy, certain he was dying. Then he heard his mother's voice.

"Shortie, get the plates. Get the plates."

He wasn't tall enough to reach the cupboard all by himself. He had to stand on his toes. He pushed himself up, getting taller, his toes digging in to the top of the rudder pedals, locking up the brakes.

Ensign Short was faintly aware of the world sliding sideways on pools of molten rubber, his canopy sliding back. Hands held his head steady, the noonday sun making him sweat, the pain in his neck telling him to wake up, wake up...

"Wake up, Ensign," the corpsman said. "Ensign Short, wake up. Sir, I'm going to slide this behind you." The corpsman inserted a stiff piece of plywood under his shoulders and neck, strapping his head in position with Velcro tape.

From the back cockpit, a disgusted fireman yelled out, "What the hell is THIS mess?"

Short answered weakly, "That's Thumper... my instructor."

"Looks more like half a buzzard."

FOURTEEN

A retired farmer named A. G. Thomas stopped his pickup truck in the middle of Conecuh County Road #6, certain that the lone hitchhiker needed help. It was nearly dark and Thumper was covered in dried blood, but A.G. picked him up anyway and drove him all the way to Evergreen.

He dropped Luke off on Liberty Street, a block away from the county sheriff's office. Before driving away, A.G. apologized for his bad manners in making a Navy man walk the whole block, but he wasn't currently on speaking terms with the sheriff and technically shouldn't be driving at all.

Following Navy tradition, Ensign Gary Short bought a round of drinks for everyone in the Officer's Club to celebrate his first flight. Then he bought another round for the crowded bar to celebrate his first landing.

And then he bought a round for his first solo. And another round for his first emergency. One more for causing enough damage during the landing to qualify as a class "A" mishap, forcing the squadron to convene a Mishap Investigation Board.

And then he bought four more beers for his date, Lieutenant Luke Harrison. His bar bill that night was over five hundred dollars. A month later, he received the Navy Air Medal for individual merit.

Lieutenant Luke Harrison bought a round of drinks for his first emergency bailout. And by popular demand, another round for abandoning ship. The JAG investigation exonerated Thumper of any wrongdoing in the incident. Six months later, the Bureau of Naval Personnel informed Lieutenant Harrison that his services as a pilot were no longer needed.

Lieutenant Ashton Cardigo received a letter of reprimand for disobeying a direct order.

The VT-6 Maintenance Officer cut off the turkey buzzard's feet and presented them to Commander Meeks, who put them on top of a high shelf in his XO's office without telling him. In a few weeks, the mysterious smell went away.

Shooter Two-Two-Five was repaired and returned to service, a bright white set of shark's teeth painted on her red and black cowling.

Avalon
Fires

Avalon Fires

Idling at the intersection of Renfroe Road, Richard got the feeling that the smartest thing to do would be to turn around and take County Road 184 all the way back home. They were still a few miles east of the Chumukla trail, but Gwen wanted to ride Renfroe Road and she wasn't in the mood to hear her husband say, "No."

She wasn't in the mood to hear him say much of anything at all. The neighbors had thrown a barbeque the previous night and Richard had decided to show off, disappearing into the garage and emerging a few minutes later with a ball of tape the size of a tennis ball with a fuse sticking out one end.

"What's that thing?" she asked.

"Sparkler bomb. Watch this." Before she could object, he pulled out a butane lighter and lit the end of the fuse. "Fire in the hole!"

Richard tossed the sizzling toy into the drainage ditch bordering their yard. The bottom of the culvert next to the mailbox was wet and muddy with runoff from the lawn sprinklers. The fuse spit and sparked, rolled over onto a wet spot and fizzled.

Everyone was tense for a few seconds, expecting a thunderous end to his experiment, but the sparkler bomb just sat there, dead. Richard watched it for almost a full minute, just to be on the safe side. "It's a dud," he confessed to his wife.

"Yeah," she agreed, "a great big dud!"

Feeling stupid, he hurried into the kitchen and got two plates of pulled pork, one for himself and one for Gwen. She was standing next to the mailbox when he came back, gossiping about husbands with two of the other wives. She took the dinner plate with a polite "thank you, baby," and pointed out that the fork was missing.

"I'll go get you one," he offered.

"Get yerself one, too!" she said. "Sometimes I think I need to remind that man to breathe." The other two women nodded.

The dead fuse in the sparkler bomb took this opportunity to draw one final breath, exhaling sparks into the tightly taped bundle. Two boxes of harmless sparklers ignited all at once, exploding with enough force to blast a shallow hole in the muck fifteen feet away from the mailbox.

Everybody spilled food. Everybody's ears rang. Bits of mud landed on the back of Gwen's neck and on top of her plate of pulled pork.

Twelve hours later, she was still moody. She wanted to ride fast, wide open, and Renfroe Road was perfectly suited to her state of mind. It was a straight half-mile of ash-white hard pack with no speed limit and no traffic. Cars couldn't get past the three-foot high speed bumps crisscrossing the road. But dirt bikes could.

~~~

Gwen gunned her blue DT-175 Enduro and dug into the first dirt mound. Richard leaned into his handlebars and fishtailed as he accelerated his red Honda 250 after her. Times like this tried his patience. He almost regretted having taught her how to ride a dirt bike. When she went out alone, he worried himself sick. He didn't breathe easy until she was home and her Yamaha was parked in the driveway.

Richard twisted the throttle as he flew over the second mound and dropped weightlessly back to the ground. Gwen was two lengths ahead. Her wheels were looking for traction, spinning, blowing dirt right into his face, tiny stones pocking his visor. He downshifted for more torque and gunned the throttle, passing the little Yamaha easily.

He glanced in his rear view and saw Gwen falling behind, rolling over the foot-high berms instead of jumping them. He had to laugh. That Yamaha she loved so much had a bum gas cap. She couldn't go all out without the cap coming loose and popping off. To keep it from rolling away, Richard had hooked a chain from the cap to the Yamaha's handlebars.

Gwen was fifty yards back, stopped completely and trying to screw the gas cap back on. Watching her husband pull so far ahead made her madder by the second. She hated losing.

Richard jumped the final dirt mound and decided to explore beyond the end of Renfroe Road. A wide puddle of standing water blocked the path, but it looked like a solid dirt trail leading around the left-hand side of the puddle. He twisted his throttle and veered left, discovering too late that hard-packed trail was actually loose silt. His skid was short and violent. Before he could react, the bike pitched forward and launched Richard face down on the other side of the puddle. He caught his breath and spit out a mouthful of dirt. His bike was laying on its side, sputtering weakly as the rear wheel spun to a halt.

Gwen was laughing as she pulled up. "You OK?" she yelled.

Richard held up his left hand. His little finger and his ring finger were bent sideways, but they straightened out as soon as he gave them a tug. "Dislocated. I need the tool kit."

Gwen untied the emergency kit behind her seat. Richard rummaged around the bag hurriedly and pulled out a set of wire cutters. "What are you gonna do with those?" Gwen asked, gasping as he aimed their jaws at the base of his ring finger. "NO!"

"I have to do this before the finger swells up."

Richard slid the wire cutters under the back of his wedding ring and snapped through the gold band. Then he cut through the other side and his ring fell off in two pieces.

The red Honda looked worse than his hand, the left side having absorbed the brunt of the crash. The rear fender was broken almost in two, the pieces connected only by a shard of fiberglass. Richard twisted it off and tossed the loose half into a shallow gully. It was ugly, but he had other problems.

The seat was bent sharply to the left, forming an "L". The mirror was missing. So were the left turn signal, the brake light, and the left foot peg. Only about two inches of clutch lever were still attached. The toe shifter was bent completely around.

Fighting off panic, he sat on the bike and rolled it back and forth. It seemed to track straight enough, so maybe there was hope. If he could manage to work the clutch lever with his two undamaged fingers, he could put his foot on the passenger's foot peg for the short ride back.

Gwen chuckled, "Looks like you're walkin' home, big boy!"

"I can ride, if we don't go too fast," he said.

"It's nearly twenty miles."

"I can do it." He had made up his mind. It was eighteen miles to their driveway. They made the trip in a little under two hours, never shifting out of second gear.

~~~

The closest bike shop was on the outskirts of Milton, but the owner had a tendency to gossip and Richard didn't fancy being the center of conversation for the rest of the summer. Gulf Breeze was farther away, but there was a shop on Red Fish

Pointe that had a good track record with motorcycle exhaust work.

Their reputation with mufflers was well deserved, but as for the rest of the bike, they turned out to be an even bet. They replaced the foot peg, the shifter, and the clutch lever, and they remounted the turn signals. But the bike mechanic could do nothing about the broken fender except trim it with a hacksaw. He fixed the bent seat by cutting it in half and covering the open end with duct tape.

Richard now owned an old, ugly bike with a shiny new muffler. He paid far more than he had originally agreed to, strapped on his helmet, and road tested his chopped-up Honda on the Garcon Point bridge. Once over Escambia Bay, he aimed the bike North up Avalon Boulevard and headed home, mentally tabulating how much money he stood to lose by selling what was left of his Honda.

He felt conspicuous riding this ugly and wounded little bike. It sounded different. It felt different. With half the saddle gone, Richard was forced to sit farther forward than usual. Strangely, the bike seemed easier to control. It was hard to tell while riding on smooth road. He needed to test it on dirt.

The next highway sign informed him that he was one mile from the junction of I-90 and Avalon Boulevard. Directly opposite the sign was an opening into a pine thicket. Richard braked hard and stood on his pegs as he carved a tight U-turn on Avalon and drove back to the hole in the woods.

The trail appeared worn but not recently used. He rolled the ugly little Honda into the woods and found a hard, flat trail that ran absolutely straight for nearly a quarter mile before turning abruptly to the left.

Richard pulled up short of the turn and stopped. It might have been his imagination, but the beat-up Honda 250 felt more self-assured than he remembered. It seemed to turn easier, to take a bigger "bite" out of the dirt. This trail went on but he decided that it would be more fun to explore the woods with Gwen.

The ride back to the road was nearly effortless. The bike looked rough and invited Richard to ride more assertively. He discovered that he actually liked its rough-shod appearance. People would underestimate what it could do. He wondered whether a coat of blue house paint would enhance the effect.

As he pulled into his driveway, Gwen was on the porch to greet him. "My God, that's one ugly Honda," she laughed as Richard slid to a stop.

~~~

They watched TV while eating breakfast off the coffee table. From Pensacola, the channel 3 Weather Watch was showing a stationary front over Mobile, giving the entire region a low overcast with a slight possibility of rain in the early afternoon. "We need it, too," the Weather Man quipped, but what would he know? The dry weather of the last four weeks had been a godsend for bikers.

"What time d'ya wanna hit the trail?" Gwen asked.

"Sometime before noon," Richard said. "If it rains at all, it'll probably happen around two o'clock or so."

"It's nearly eleven," she said.

"Well, I'm ready to go now!" He swallowed the last bite of a jelly-and-bacon sandwich and grabbed his boots.

"You'll have to wait. I'm not ready," she said. "I'm not a man. I wasn't born ready."

"I'll see ya outside, then."

Men could be so infuriating, especially Richard, but he had to be forgiven. He simply didn't understand girl stuff. Her clothes had to look good in the mirror long before they got soaked in mud. She tried on her pink jacket, changed her mind, and then changed it again. Ten minutes later, she was finally satisfied that blue jeans, a t-shirt, a denim jacket, and motocross boots would look Just Right with Nirvana Peach lip gloss.

Richard had already rolled her Yamaha into the middle of the driveway. She sat on it and pulled out the choke, watching him push his battle-scarred Honda out of the garage.

"Try to keep that rat-ugly muck bucket outa the puddles today, OK sweetie?" she said. Two kicks later, her slender Yamaha spat a cold cloud of oily smoke. She nursed it along with the throttle, waiting for the two-stroke motor to warm up.

The ugly Honda sparked to life on the first kick.

"Good omen," Richard said.

"Well, let's put it to use. Show me this great new trail of yours."

He looked at the sky. The clouds formed a solid, flat base as far as he could see. They were low, too. "Might rain," he said.

"Might not. C'mon, let's ride."

Richard sniffed the air. "Doesn't smell like rain. Clouds look wet, but I don't smell rain."

"So can we ride?"

"I think we got a couple of hours before this storm hits."

"I'm ready," she growled.

"Then quit screwin' around. Let's go."

Five minutes south of Milton on I-90, they banked left and picked up the black asphalt of Avalon Boulevard. A rustic Texaco station sat on the corner, a whitewashed wooden shack with two pumps sitting out in the open air, its parking lot empty. The architecture of the old station doomed it to eventual failure. Nobody ever bought gas from a country store any more.

Richard and Gwen both looked at the station as they drove by. The trailhead they were looking for was a mile farther down the road. Dense pine plantations lined either side of Avalon. Richard pulled over into the right-of-way and shut down his Honda, the front wheel pointing into the hole in the trees. The Yamaha pulled up on his left and its engine clattered to a stop.

"Is this it?" Gwen asked.

"Yeah. You gonna follow me, or do you wanna lead?"

"I'll follow," she said, turning in her seat and looking back down the road.

"What're you looking at?"

"That gas station. I really should top off."

"We won't be riding that long," Richard said. "Look at the clouds. First sign of rain and we're outa here!"

The gray overcast was moving like a conveyor belt, smoothly gliding in from the west at an eerie, unchanging pace. There were no breaks in the cloud cover, not even any fluffy wisps of scud…just the featureless bottom of an endless, distant storm.

The two bikers cautiously advanced through the hollow into the woods. Once inside, they stood on their pegs and let their motors run at an easy strain. The first quarter mile was exactly as Richard remembered – a fast ride.

The trees brushed by, closer and closer, and the trail narrowed, forcing the riders to slow down. Abruptly, it turned sharply to the right and pointed north.

For five hundred yards, the dirt path ran perpendicular to the rows of pines, all planted in perfectly straight lines. And where it traversed a row of trees, the ground rose and fell in a gentle slope.

Richard's throttle hand couldn't resist so obvious a challenge. It twisted a bit more fuel into the Honda's motor as the bike crested one of the shallow humps. One jump led to another, and then another. Four, five, then six more, each one spaced identically apart.

And suddenly, a solid wall of trees blocked their way. The trail broke hard to the left, running parallel to its original course.

Richard saw the turn just in time and slid to the left to intercept its centerline. Gwen twisted her Enduro left, let him pull away and then followed fifty feet back.

The footing was uneven and rocky, the path turning to the right so imperceptibly that the bikers barely noticed they had changed direction back to the north, again. They worked on keeping their bikes moving forward.

The nature of the trail changed unexpectedly, as though it had passed through an invisible door, opening up on the other side, becoming straight and wide and easy. Gwen noticed tracks in the sand, deep and far apart. "Cars have been here," she thought.

The neat and orderly pines gave way to random hardwoods, scrubby oak and maple interspersed with dead limbs left over from a clear-cutting harvest. There were new pines already planted in the cutover, but they wouldn't peek over the rotting logs for another year.

The tracks dipped low into a dry gully, then climbed uphill and stopped on a grassy shoulder bordering a two-lane highway. They had made it to the other side. Their ride was over. Richard shut down and waited for Gwen to catch up.

"Any idea where we are?" he asked. There were no road signs visible in either direction.

Gwen looked up at the sky, watched the clouds for a second and said, "It's I-90."

"How do you figure that?"

"We were going south on Avalon before we got onto the trail, and now we're heading north," she explained. "I-90 is the only road north of where we were."

"Damn shame. I was just starting to have fun. I don't want to go home, yet."

"Well, we can always go straight," Gwen said, pointing across the road. "It looks like the trail keeps going."

Directly across the road stood a thick forest of pine. Not the neat rows of a pine plantation like they had just explored, but a mix of young and old natural trees growing together into a wall of solid evergreen, seemingly impenetrable. Richard and Gwen both spotted faint tracks leading across the soft dirt shoulder and disappearing into a dark hollow – a door into the woods.

"I'll go look," Richard said, starting his Honda.

"I will, too!"

Together they rolled across I-90 and headed directly to the dark hollow. As soon as each biker pulled within a dozen feet of the dark hollow they could see what lay beyond. First the Honda, then the Yamaha, disappeared into the woods, following a trail barely wide enough to walk on.

Once through the door, the trail became a tunnel, claustrophobic and breezeless. The ground was soft and yielding, sucking at their tires and threatening to glue them in place. Not many people had ever passed this way. Tiny limbs stuck out into the trail, grabbing and poking at exposed skin.

The path was straight and apparently man-made, but Richard wondered at the sanity of a trail that was so long, without any way to turn around. He kept an eye on Gwen in his mirror. She was pacing him from a workable distance.

Progress was slow, and what little there was cost the riders sweat, strained muscles, and gasoline. Without saying it, they both wished they had stopped back at the Texaco station.

The scenery didn't change, but their speed did. They slowed. Tree after tree crept by as they forced the bikes deeper into the woods.

Gwen kept an eye on the clouds. They were her compass, flowing from the west toward the east. The clouds told her that they were driving due north. Watching the clouds made her feel less lost, but the overcast had taken on an ominous, rolling form. She thought the it looked lower, or maybe it was just moving faster. Had the wind picked up? It was impossible to tell.

The air inside the burrow tasted hot and stale. Between the trees, clumps of grass and weeds choked off any possibility of leaving the thin trail they were on. They fought to gain a few feet, a few yards. A half hour later they were deeper inside the tunnel and still fighting for inches.

Ten yards ahead, she could just make out the clumsy-looking Honda digging a trench as its tires spun and sprayed dirt. Working her own clutch and throttle, Gwen fought off the irrational fear that the trail would just stop, no way forward, no way back. She caught herself craving speed and wind and water and gasoline and cheap gas station food.

Up ahead, there seemed to more sunlight on the path. A few seconds later, Gwen followed Richard into an opening not much bigger than their garage.. The one-way trail was suddenly flat and hard and wide enough for three bikes. He turned to Gwen and said the obvious, "Wow! I thought we'd NEVER get out of there!"

They both sat for a moment, decompressing from their trip through the tunnel. Richard got off his ugly Honda, left it idling, and walked down the new pathway, disappearing around a curve to the left. A moment later, he came back, pausing to examine a small opening in the trees to their right.

He climbed back on his bike. "Well... it's an old, old road. Footing is pretty good, but there's no telling where it goes."

"What choice do we have?" Gwen asked.

"Oh, we got a choice. We can turn around and spend another hour going back the way we came. Or, if you prefer, we can go that way." He pointed at the small space to their right. "But I just looked in there and it looks like the same deer trail we've been following."

Gwen squinted at the new, narrow tunnel. "I'm in the mood to get some breeze."

"OK, let's see what happens on the big road." He popped into first gear and skidded off down the open trail, curving left and disappearing.

A hundred yards in, the curve widened slightly. Still, it kept turning, endlessly left and left and left. Gwen glanced at the sky and saw that the curve had turned them completely around from north to south. Then the road spilled out into a small field, dotted with young volunteer pines and littered with twenty or thirty old stoves, washing machines, and toilet bowls.

"It's a dump!" Richard yelled.

"Yeah, well that means that this road goes somewhere. Maybe it leads home. Let's go!"

They cranked up together and raced through the junkyard side-by-side, jockeying for advantage. Richard's Honda had the edge in horsepower, but it was only a slight edge and the ugly bike had to carry more weight than Gwen's Yamaha. At the edge of the dump, she pulled away easily, her two-cycle engine screaming like a mad chainsaw.

Richard didn't mind being in second place. Gwen was a good rider, competent and strong. And there was just something about a girl on a motorcycle. Watching her move was like pouring a glass of water on the desert. There was always room for more.

The old road bent to the right a little and then straightened out, inviting the bikers to shift up to the next gear. The trees blurred past on both sides and the sky slid sideways in a disorienting visual argument. Then the road narrowed and became a trail, then a skinny path, and then it stopped completely – another dead end against another forest of wild pine. Gwen shut down her engine and pulled off her helmet. Richard pulled alongside and stared at the wall of trees.

Gwen twisted in her saddle. "Where are we?"

"I don't know," Richard said. "I'm all turned around. The trail is older than the woods. I'm sorry, Gwen."

"Well, I wanna go home." She sagged against her handlebars. "I guess we have to go back through that godawful skinny trail."

"Afraid so."

"Lead out, then."

Richard spun around to the right. With Gwen following far enough back to stay out of his dirt spray, he crept up to thirty, then thirty-five, pulling well ahead and banking into a tight turn that would take him through the appliance dump.

~~~

Gwen was focused on the ruts in the trail directly in front of her and she lost sight of the lead bike. She shot past the turnoff, but out of the corner of her eye caught a glimmer of a red taillight in the distance. Slamming on her brake, she locked the handlebars hard over to the left and leaned against the turn as she swapped ends at full power and entered the trail nearly a hundred yards behind Richard.

She couldn't see the Honda, and the only engine sound was her own. Gwen peered ahead through her goggles, trying hard to see where he had gone when a brilliant blue flash exploded in the dirt ten feet in front of her tire. The concussion showered her with dirt.

The first thing she thought of was one of Richard's big, homemade firecrackers – his idea of a joke. She was hot, tired, left behind, and now angry. Throwing fireworks was not funny. That man of hers would pay, and pay dearly... just as soon as she caught him!

~~~

Out of sight, Richard was just entering the appliance dump when he heard the rattling staccato of a full automatic weapon, loud and unmistakable – "POP-POP-POP-POP-POP." Dirt flew up as tracers ripped a line across the trail in front of him.

"Marijuaneros," he thought. A moment later, he realized that Gwen wasn't behind him anymore. He had to warn her. He had to stop.

Still within gun range, Richard skidded the Honda sideways and laid the bike all the way down, sliding to a stop against the ground. He pressed his body into the dirt as flat as he could make it, using the bike as cover. He couldn't stay there long without getting shot, but Gwen was riding into an ambush and this was the only way he could warn her. He heard the Yamaha's engine straining, speeding into view... and into the line of fire.

~~~

She flew recklessly into the clearing and immediately saw him on the ground behind his bike. She was still furious, thinking that the fool got what he deserved, but then she noticed a strange urgency to his gestures. Over the sound of her engine she thought she heard Richard yelling something about "shooting".

Reducing the throttle but still rolling, Gwen looked around the junkyard. Several small fires were burning randomly around the field. The hairs on the back of her neck stiffened when she realized what was happening. Gwen kicked her bike into the next gear, accelerating through the junkyard to the safety of the trail on the far side.

~~~

Richard watched her power out of the junkyard, glad that she was safe. The next volley of fire would cut him down, and the Honda gave him virtually no protection. He couldn't afford to lay around any more.

He picked up the ugly little bike and, in a single fluid motion, leaped onto the seat and kicked the starter. Its engine popped to life on the first try. Richard squeezed the clutch, prayed and snapped the foot lever into first gear.

He was taking too long, but the marijuaneros weren't shooting any more. He wondered why. He was too good a target to pass up. Had he imagined it? He looked around the clearing. Where the tracers had hit, small fires were burning… growing larger, merging, and picking up the wind. He wondered just then why pot growers would use tracers. Why would they shoot at all? It made no sense.

A brilliant flash to the south and the "POP" of electricity hitting the ground gave Richard the answer. A storm was upon them… a dry storm, crackling with lightning.

~~~

Richard's nose picked up a heavy, dry odor. The side of the clearing where he and Gwen had come in was obscured by as light haze that hadn't been there a minute before. In seconds the haze billowed and thickened, gray-white. Light smoldering sheets of blowing smoke swiftly turned dark, blotting out the tree line beyond. Richard watched as the dark gray curtain began to glow orange from behind. The fire superheated the dense smoke and converted the onrushing blackness into a blistering hell.

Accelerating away from the heat, he hurried to join Gwen. She had already made the turnaround and sat at the entrance to the skinny one-way trail. She waved him over and sniffed the air. "Is that smoke?" she asked.

"Yeah, it's coming from the dump."

"No, too far away. The dump is just a coupla little fires."

"Not any more. We have to get going right now and this damn tunnel is the only way out." He gunned his throttle twice, a signal that he was ready to go.

"No, wait!" she stopped him. "Something's not right. Something's ..."

Deep down the one-way trail, a bright flicker caught her attention. Then another, softer orange and distant.

"...fire? Fire! Oh, God. Richard, the woods are burning down there. We're trapped!"

"We have to make a run for it through there," he said, pointing to the small deer trail they had passed on the way in. "Stay right on my tail!"

"You just get us outa here, don't worry 'bout me!" she yelled.

Richard spun the Honda in a half-doughnut and raced ahead. Drifting smoke wrapped around him, consumed him, hiding him from Gwen. She watched him disappear and felt a stabbing paranoia that she would never see him again. Shocked into action, she pushed her Yamaha hard, laying against her tank to pass under a low-hanging branch. She didn't relax until he was once again in view.

The deer trail opened up slightly about fifty yards inside the wood. Flat, hard ground, speckled with saplings and volunteer pines, carried the riders in a twisting line. Smoke filtered through the woods, burning Gwen's eyes and nose.

The trail banked sharply to the right, opened wider and ran straight, a welcome change. Level ground invited higher speeds, but in the haze they were already moving too fast. Gwen saw Richard snap his head to the left. Reflexively, she looked over in the same direction.

Fire was blasting through the underbrush fifty yards off their flank. Pushed by the wind, it was gnawing at the dried fuel, growing and spitting hot embers ahead of the fire line.

Gwen stayed on Richard's bumper as he picked up speed to get ahead of the blaze. They were faster than the flames, but just barely. By the time the bikes arrived at the end of the straightaway, they had raced the fire for nearly a quarter mile. Now, barely fifty yards ahead of the flames, the trail turned sharply left.

Richard hoped Gwen was still close on his tail as he jinked left and gunned his throttle, hoping for enough speed to beat the wave of fire rushing toward the trail.

The trail conspired to slow them down. The footing was soft and narrow, robbing their tires of traction and cutting their speed and pilfering valuable seconds. Small pines whistled and screamed as the fire boiled off their sap and ignited their waxy needles. The riders were losing ground as the blaze ran straight at them, a storm of brilliant orange sparks showering ahead of the flames.

Bogged down in the soft dirt, Richard struggled to get traction and skitter across the surface tension. Gwen waited behind him, transfixed at the sight of Hell rushing at them.

Richard jumped straight up and let his full weight fall on the saddle as he downshifted, driving his rear tire deep into the sand. The tread took a bite, throwing a rooster tail of loose dirt and jetting forward in a neck-wrenching lurch.

His trench tried to swallow Gwen's tires but she was ready for it, attacking the sand in second gear, leaning back to get the weight off her front wheel. As soon as she felt the bike tilt backward, she gunned the throttle. Her rear wheel torqued forward briskly, giving her the speed her life depended on.

Then she heard herself scream. She didn't intend to scream, and didn't immediately realize the sound was coming from her own throat.

A burning ember, glowing red, was stuck to her shirtsleeve, etching into the flesh of her left arm. She couldn't stop, not now. She had to just put up with the agonizing speck on her arm and screaming helped. So she screamed and screamed again, more from anger than fear. Her nostrils burned from the blowing smoke and her ears ached from the roar of the Yamaha's engine and the inferno threatening to sweep over their heads.

The trail bent left, then right, in a wide, sweeping arc. The ground firmed up inside the curve and the two bikes leaped ahead of the fire. The furious blaze howled at them, licked at them, and then let them go, for now.

~ ~ ~

The air felt cooler. The smell of smoke was finally gone. The trail was clear and solid. Richard felt safer now that they were ahead of the fire, but the trees bordering the new trail kept them moving east. They were being ushered in one direction and he didn't like that. He kept hoping for an escape route.

But at least the road was clear and straight and flat. Any minute now, they'd pop out onto asphalt and be on the road home. East... east. "Where would that put us?" he wondered. Before he had an answer, the trail narrowed. Before long he was crawling along in first gear, again, Gwen close behind.

The slow progress was infuriating. The trail started drifting to the left in a shallow turn, and then it curved back to the right. Richard made the turn and stopped. Gwen pulled in tightly behind him.

"I am completely lost," he said.

She looked up at the clouds and frowned. "We're pointed north, sort of. Any idea where this all comes out?"

"None at all." He shut down the Honda's engine and Gwen killed hers as well. Richard tried not to dwell on what would happen if the bikes wouldn't start again. They were in a quiet cocoon in the woods, the soothing tick-tink of the hot engines strangely out of context in the middle of a forest fire.

Richard got off and looked around. He could hear the fire's thunder in the distance and was about to pat Gwen on the arm when he saw her burnt sleeve and the red, exposed flesh inside.

"Gwen, you're hurt!"

"Yeah, it got a little hot back there. It doesn't hurt, yet, but it will soon. I'd give anything for an asphalt road."

Richard held her arm and examined the burn. It was bad. She needed to be in an ER, not in the damn woods! Something behind him got his attention. Gwen saw him freeze and tilt his head to the side. He quickly did an about-face, staring up the trail, his eyes wide.

"What?" Gwen asked.

"Sshhh!" He held up one finger.

She waited for a few seconds before interrupting again. "What? What is it?"

Richard jumped on his bike and started it with a single, emphatic kick. "Let's go, we gotta move…hurry!"

Before she could ask again, Richard was already blasting up the trail. She started the Yamaha on the third kick and fell in behind him.

The way ahead was clear. For fifty yards, she wondered whether Richard had lost his mind. She smelled smoke, faintly, but it was impossible to see the source… NO! There it was! Off to her right, a broad wave of burning underbrush, spitting and hissing. It was downwind, moving away from them.

She looked at it for a second and almost missed seeing him stop in the middle of the trail. Staring at the fire, he turned toward Gwen and smiled. "We got lucky. We're upwind." He slipped into first gear and continued pushing north. Richard slowed to a safer speed and pressed on for another five minutes.

They broke out into a small sandy clearing, rising in the middle to form a low hill, about six feet high in the middle. Gangly oaks randomly surrounded the hill, but there were no pines or saplings. From the top of the hill, the trees and the stark, grassless surface defined a rough circle fifty yards across where almost nothing grew.

"What is this place?" Gwen asked.

"A burial ground. We're on top of a toxic waste pit."

"Like what? What kind of waste?"

"Paint cans, asbestos siding, dead cattle, engine oil. Everything unpleasant."

"What's it doing way out here?"

Richard had the answer in half a second. "There's a farm nearby," he said. "Oh, babe, we're almost out of the woods!"

Beyond the hill, there was no trail. It looked as though their escape was going to end badly. Gwen looked around and noticed a swampy low spot half-hidden by reeds. She looked again and discovered a broad footpath that led around the bog.

Richard hurried on to see what was on the other side of the swamp. The mud sucked at his bike, his tires hurling specks and chunks of dark gray mud back at Gwen.

She paused to give her husband more working room, and to get a better look at the swamp. It was actually the shallow end of a finger lake that stretched a few hundred yards to the west.

She was about to get moving again and was letting out her clutch when Richard suddenly shot past her, going in the opposite direction.

Richard stopped and yelled, "Burning! Just north of the water, the fire is blocking the trail."

"What do we do?"

"There's only one thing we can do. Get back to the clearing and hunker down. Wait it out."

Gwen didn't like the idea. "That's suicide! If the fires build up around that place, the heat and smoke... we'll suffocate!"

"What other choice do we have?"

Gwen thought for a moment. "We get off this trail and run for the far end of the lake."

"What?"

"Look," she explained, "we're out of options. This is a lake. People go fishing on it... maybe there's a road they use."

"Okay! Go, go!" He waved her into the lead.

Gwen gunned her Yamaha and aimed it along the shoreline, trying hard to keep her wheels on dry ground. There was precious little that was dry, though. The edge of the bog dragged at her tires and thorns tore her pants.

The underbrush closed in around her, trapping her in a briar-lined net. "Go back!" she yelled at Richard.

He flicked the ugly Honda into neutral and pushed it backwards, looking for a place to turn around. He saw an opening in the briars on his left, thrust forward into the space and found himself on a wide hiking trail less than five yards away.

Gwen soon pulled up alongside him. "Good. You found an actual trail."

"Yeah, you were right," he said. "How's the arm?"

"Still doesn't hurt. We got other...fish...to," her voice trailed off. She had picked up a change in the air. It felt cooler, but the smoke was getting thicker and worse, it was coming from the wrong direction.

"We gotta move," she said. "The wind has shifted!"

The cold air fed fresh oxygen to the fires. Downwind, the blaze swapped ends, found new fuel lying on the ground and exploded with renewed fury. The hot smoke reached the riders within seconds.

Richard punched the Honda into first gear and started tearing at the footpath. A hundred yards farther, the path opened wide and the riding was easier, but the smoke was thicker and burned his eyes. The fire to the south was moving much faster than the bikes and its flames were pulling ahead on their left. Like pincers, the two fires would soon trap them.

Slaloming around the trees near the shoreline, they both saw it at the same time. Connecting the two sides of the lake at the halfway point, the bridge was old, wooden and twisted. But it was undeniably a bridge.

Richard locked his rear brake and skidded to a stop at the bridgehead. The wooden planks were broken in places and covered in moss near the edges. There were no hand rails.

"Is it safe?" she asked.

"Compared to what?"

"How far is the drop? Y'know, into the lake?" Her voice quivered, then she coughed. Smoke was coming in from behind, engulfing them. The smoke was already hot, ready to ignite any second, now. Richard shook her handlebars to get her attention, yelling, "Go!"

She trusted that he would follow, but her rear view mirrors had both been bent inward by the swamp briars. She thought she heard the ugly red Honda's four-stroke growl, but it was drowned out by the dull roar of exploding fire-front smoke. Terrified, she concentrated on the bridge ahead.

The first ten yards were the easiest. Gwen put her feet down and baby-stepped her bike down the bridge. Trying to move delicately, her bike rattled the wooden planks ahead of her and two of them shook off. She decided to risk picking her feet up and found it easier to stay in the center than she thought it would be.

A rotted plank cracked as her rear tire rolled over it. Instinctively, she touched the brakes and stopped. The cracked board took the full weight of her tire and snapped in two. The tire dropped into the space and caught the boards on either side of the missing one.

Gwen heard another crack beneath her bike. Without thinking about it, she popped her clutch and jumped forward out of the hole and back to the center of the bridge.

Going slowly, she fought to keep her bike away from the edge, flirting with a six-foot drop into a shallow pond lined with dead trees. Falling off the bridge meant sharing the black water with poisonous snakes, chased into the cool lake by the burning underbrush. Gwen tried not to think about the water moccasins, coral snakes, and pygmy rattlers writhing angrily just beneath the surface. She forced herself to focus.

Halfway across, the bridge sagged about six inches on the right-hand side. The planks in the sag were slick with fungus. Gwen knew that the faster she hit the slippery spot, the safer she'd be.

Fifteen yards was not a lot of room to accelerate, so she popped the Yamaha into second gear and opened the throttle all the way. The little two-stroke engine was tired and hot, the cylinders pinging under the stress. She aimed as far left as she could, to stay away from the sagging boards.

She hit the high side of the droop at a little over twenty miles an hour. The rear tire spun as it touched the slimy surface, skidding to the right and slipping down toward the mossy drop off. She felt the bike slipping out of control and decided that, if she was going to fall into the water, she was going to hit it as fast as she could.

Gwen twisted the throttle fully open, the engine singing under the strain as the rear tire spun, looking for traction. The tire hit the raised edge of the bridge, a wooden lip slightly more than an inch high.

It was enough. The rubber grabbed clean wood and propelled the Yamaha forward a foot, away from the surface moss and onto good, dry boards. Ignoring the pain in her left arm, she guided her bike down the centerline for the remaining fifty yards.

Gwen didn't exhale until both tires were once again on solid ground. She stood on the rear brake and spun around to face the bridge, hoping to see Richard but afraid to look.

The ugly Honda accelerated past the final twenty feet with its front wheel inches off the surface of the old bridge. Richard was hanging on for the ride, fishtailing as he braked to a stop. He was holding his breath, too, exhaling only when he was next to Gwen.

She smiled. "That was fun! Let's do it again!"

He let the quip go by. "Look there," he said, pointing at an old, wide vehicle path. It was overgrown with saw grass, but the tracks were unmistakable, straight and wide. Hopeful, Richard rolled down the trail and Gwen followed.

Less then fifty yards later, the trail ended on the edge of a tantalizing, wide open hay field, the season's first cutting lying dry on the ground. The land was flat and wide and completely without trees. But the best part sat on the far side of the pasture, five hundred feet away, the most beautiful sight they had seen all day…a fire truck.

But between the riders and the hay field were five strands of fresh, new barbed wire.

"All we need to do is get from here to there," Richard said.

"Though this." Gwen plucked the taut upper strand. Whoever had put it here knew what they were doing.. Her eyes searched up and down the fence line, hoping in vain for a gate.

"Give me the tool kit." Richard fumbled with the bungees holding the bag in place behind her seat. It took too long, but he finally pulled out the wire cutters.

He knelt by the fence and bit into the bottom wire with the jaws of the cutter. He squeezed hard but only made a small dent on the twisted wire. He switched hands and tried again.

Gwen held the wire while Richard's tool gnawed at it, but the wire was too strong. Several minutes later, the bottom wire finally gave way and snapped.

"This is horrible," he said. "My arms hurt and these cutters aren't made to cut through fence like this. It'll take forever."

"Rich, baby, we don't have forever." Gwen pointed to the far right edge of the pasture. Smoke was just beginning to blow across the fence and onto the hay field. Two small deer

appeared through the smoke and bolted over the fence,
propelled by terror.

"Oh, Christ," Richard said. "Help me cut this next wire."
He pushed the next strand into the jaws of cutter and squeezed
as hard as he could. The barbed wire wouldn't give. Richard
put the cutter handles between his knees and used his thigh
muscles to supplement his hands.

Gwen watched as fire blossomed through the fence.
"Richard, hurry!" she urged.

Snap!

Richard held up the cutting pliers. One of the handles had
broken off. The barbed wire was still intact.

"Oh, Rich. What are we going to do?"

Richard looked at the fire, which was licking at the field of
drying hay. The pasture was too wide and the burning grass
fire was moving too fast to outrun it on foot. He looked at the
one strand of barbed wire that he actually did manage to cut.

He walked around behind Gwen and shoved her bike over,
letting it fall to the ground. Gwen objected, "Hey!"

Richard did the same thing to his ugly red Honda.

"We go under."

Richard helped Gwen cross under the wire, then he
followed. He reached under the one broken wire and grabbed
the Yamaha's front wheel. Grunting, the two of them slid the
little bike under the fence, into the field.

Smoke billowed up from the south. The fires behind them
had jumped the lake and would soon burst though the trail and
feed on the drying hay. Gwen took the time to put her bike on
its kickstand, then helped Richard pull the ugly Honda under
the wire.

"Richard, I smell gas," she said.

He sniffed the air and nodded his head. "Gwen! Your cap
is off!"

She scrambled to close off the filler neck, but could only
find the chain. The cap was gone, pulled off when they
dragged her bike under the fence.

Richard frantically searched the grass by the fence. Gwen was watching the flames advancing on them. "No time," she told him. "I'll have to ride without a cap."

"No! Gas will blow out all over you. Here, use this," he said, balling up his shirt and stuffing as much of it as possible into the filler hole.

"Looks like a Molotov cocktail," she laughed. Richard glared at her. Her joke wasn't funny. He picked up the Honda and got it running with two sharp kicks.

Gwen was on her fifth kick and the Yamaha still wouldn't start. Flames were visible coming up the lakeside trail. "Richard," she stated calmly, "get out of here. I'll be along in a minute. It's flooded or something."

"You can't stay here…"

"…I can't get it to start and running is too slow…"

"…I'm not leaving you behind."

"If you stay here you'll burn, too. You have to get out of here," she screamed at him.

"Sorry, babe. It doesn't work like that." He shut down the Honda and walked over to where she was.

Gwen was in tears. "Oh, hell! We almost made it!"

He reached for her handlebars and said, "No, I meant it won't work like that. You have to do this first." He turned her ignition key from "Off" to "On".

The Yamaha started it on the first kick. Richard slapped her on the back and yelled, "Now move!" Gwen pulled away, heading straight for the fire truck on the other side of the field. She watched the fresh blaze rushing at her from the right. She figured they could make it across and beat the flames, but it would be close.

Five fast seconds later, they were both in the path of the blaze. The wind had freshened, pushing the fire faster across the open hay field. Gwen saw the flames leap and lick at the air and gain ground. "Faster!" she told herself. Risking unseen armadillo holes, stumps and ditches, she twisted the throttle to eke a little more speed, just a little.

Without a sputter, her engine quit dead.

Richard pulled alongside. "WHAT'S WRONG?" he yelled over the roar of the blaze that was headed their way.

Gwen pulled the shirt out of the gas filler and rocked her bike back and forth.

"EMPTY!" she shouted back.

Richard got off of the ugly Honda and let it fall. He pointed at the fire and yelled one word at her, but she couldn't hear it over the crackling roar of the fire eating the hay field. She didn't need to hear the word. She could read his lips.

"RUN!"

She dropped her bike where it was and sprinted toward the road, a hundred yards away. Richard stayed behind her in case she fell, but she had always been the better runner. Embers showered down around them, starting new fires in their footprints and scorching Richard's shirtless back.

In the distance, the ugly little Honda's gas tank overheated and popped. Richard didn't need to look back, even if the fire would let him. He knew what the sound was, and felt a little sadness in the midst of the terror.

There wasn't much time to dwell on the burning Honda. Fire was blowing in from their right, and the wave of flame rushed past them, behind them, and in front, surrounding them both and beginning to feast. Gwen slowed to a stop and shrugged.

Richard stopped with her and looped his arms around her shoulders. Wheezing dizzily in the smoke, their skin felt strangely cool. Water droplets, big ones, were raining down sideways against their faces. Not rain. Hitting too hard to be rain.

Voices by the road shouted at them, "Run... run!"

Gwen and Richard both heard the firemen and felt the water from their hose at nearly the same moment, but the fire surrounding them was hotter and more powerful than the hose. A second hose opened, then a third, all them drenching the field just in front of the bikers.

Stumbling and heavy from the water, they ran past the pumper truck and caught their breath by the side of the road.

Richard counted six more fire trucks speeding east. The fire crew that had showered them was now busy trying to save a barn.

"I don't think we're going to get a ride with these guys," Gwen said. "Any idea where we are?"

"I think this is Hamilton Bridge Road. We're about ten miles from home. Wanna walk? Maybe we can hitch."

"You know nobody is gonna pick up a couple of wet hitchhikers," she said.

"A nice walk will do us good."

Richard set out at a slow, comfortable pace. Gwen found it easy to keep up. They headed east, into a clean wind. Her hand found his and their fingers twisted gently together.

Coward's Song

Coward's Song

No man knows for certain whether he's a coward. I didn't discover the truth until a rainy Friday in June.

As summers went, this one started out oppressively humid. The forecast had promised cooling rains but the morning delivered only a hot blue sky. The air conditioning in our cramped, three-story townhouse couldn't push cold air above the second floor, leaving the third floor bedroom joylessly hot and uninhabitable. We survived only because the cool first-floor den had a large couch.

There was precious little relief from the heat at work. My office was a narrow alcove with a circular window overlooking the parking lot thirty feet below. Square clean spots on the walls testified to its previous life as a storeroom. Two other writers sweltered in there with me.

That Friday, I sat on the windowsill, eating lunch and watching a bank of low gray clouds drifting over the Potomac. The monotony of the windless heat made sleep irresistible. I closed my eyes for a brief moment and was enjoying a quiet dream of mountain air.

The sky cracked open with an explosive bolt through a nearby tree, shaking the entire building awake. Rain hammered at the alcove window and the parking lot below. I stood at the window and stared. The storm's sudden cold fury was spellbinding.

My phone rang, urgently. My wife, shouting to be heard, had bad news. Water was pouring in. The basement was flooding.

"COME HOME!"

~~~

The highways were crowded and wet. Normally a half-hour drive, the distance had doubled overnight. The entire way home was further slowed by blinding downpours in which I could not see fifty feet ahead and I couldn't shake the disheartening realization that the tractor trailer coming up behind me had the same visibility.

The temptation to pull over and wait for the storm to pass was dulled by a decade of marital harmony predicated on the notion that the later I showed up to help, the more the storm became my fault. I mulled the option to run away and become an elephant tender but ultimately decided to go home anyway.

I parked in front of our living room and inspected the situation from the comfort of the driver's seat. The parking lot met the townhouse on its second floor. Two stories up, rain cascaded down the roof and into the gutter. Halfway to the drainpipe, a nearly solid stream spilled over the edge of the gutter, directly into our sunken basement window.

Water stood more than a foot deep on the outside of the glass. It leaked in through the hinges and pooled on the floor, threatening to overflow into the den.

There was no time to change clothes. I sprinted around the row of townhouses and into my own, generous back yard. I slowed down rounding the turn through the open gate, but not enough, discovering that science had given up on adding friction to dress shoes. I slid through the gate on a single buttock, heading straight for the fence and the twenty-foot extension ladder hung thereon months earlier. A catastrophic impact was averted at the final instant when I was slowed to a stop by a pair of well-endowed rose bushes.

I had bought the ladder a year earlier, hoping to save money by painting the townhouse myself. At the time, I had been unaware of the foul temperament of extension ladders.

Reaching over the thorns and lifting the ladder off its hooks, I was reminded of that dry, sunny day that I dared fate and climbed aloft with brush and bucket in hand. Pulleys and ropes dangled and twisted, snatching at my feet. Every time I moved, ladder danced and sashayed. With my every breath, the rungs would creak, their metallic popping amplified by my suffocating fear. My hands would not move. My body was locked in place. My mind was in a strange land on the far side of terror, beyond self-control.

It took my wife half an hour to talk me down from six feet up. I hung the ladder on the fence and left it there. During cookouts, guests would point and say, "Sooo... ya got yerself an extension ladder."

"Yup... she's a twenty-footer," I'd proudly say, as if I scaled its satanic heights every morning and danced on the top blindfolded.

A year later, it groaned disagreeably as I hauled it on my shoulders to the front of the townhouse. Cold and slippery, it was heavier than I remembered. Twice, I slipped and fell on the wet grass. It was the ladder's fault. I didn't pause to reprimand the mutinous beast.

I set it upright on my lawn and after a brief struggle, pulled the ladder open, stretching it as tall as it would go. But something was wrong.

I was out of breath and the ladder wasn't as tall as it had been a year ago. At its highest point it was a full four feet short of the rain gutter. I was going to have to stand near the top rung. My wife saw the predicament and came outside into the downpour and offered to help steady the legs.

I should have said "No." I wanted to say "No." Instead, I quietly asked God to take away the fear just this one time.

Rain pelted me from above and the waterfall gushing from the rain gutter arced out into the air and past my shoulder, barely a foot away. I gave my wet wife a weak smile, put on my Brave Face, and climbed. With each rung, I told myself that it's only a ladder, that *normal* people do this sort of thing every day. The higher I climbed, the less normal I felt.

Halfway up, the ladder's thin aluminum frame started to swing lazily back and forth under my weight. I glanced down and saw my wife looking off to her side. The rain was stinging her eyes so badly she couldn't look up. Unable to see what I was doing above her, she was no longer steadying the ladder.

My hands were paralyzed. How strange, I thought. I could wiggle my fingers but I couldn't make them release their grip on the rung above me. My feet slipped from side to side, and I marveled at the wrongness of deciding to rush up the ladder in waterlogged dress shoes.

I fought my panic and moved one up rung. Then I paused while my grip relaxed and I recovered from the dread of being one foot higher. Then another rung - climb, pause, relax. Soon, my eyes were even with the bottom of the second-floor bedroom window.

The dry, warm bedroom. I wanted to go inside and take a nap – just a short rest – but my left foot slipped sideways and I found myself back on the ladder, welded in place.

I gripped the rung above me so tightly that my arm went numb. I couldn't breathe. My chest hurt. I had read about heart attacks. I steeled myself for the sternum-clutching death fall, the wind whistling in my ears as gravity pulled me faster and faster to my final rest, fifteen feet below.

In the bedroom window's reflection was a man I didn't recognize. His face was distorted by terror. He was a coward.

I was a coward.

Shame forced my hands to pull me up three more rungs. I could go no higher. I was at the top, and yet the gutter was still above my head, water sloshing over its side in torrents. Trembling, I reached up as far as my arm would stretch and grabbed the metal rim, testing it to see if it could hold my weight.

The thin sheet metal bent outward, too flimsy to hold me even for a second. My fear boiled. I carefully worked my way back down the ladder. Down, all the way down, feeling wetter and safer and more ashamed by the foot. "What's wrong?" my wife shouted over the thundering rain.

"I can't reach the gutter!" I yelled back.

"You *have* to! We don't have any other choice."

I looked at the neighbor's townhouse. Their roof slanted down more than ours did. I pointed up at it and shouted, "I can use their roof to get higher up!"

We lifted our ladder and moved it next door, resting it against their brown shingle roof. There was no time to ask for permission. By the time the neighbors found out what we had done, the coroner would be finished with me and my wife would be a widow. She ran back into the basement to bail water, an increasingly hopeless task.

I went up the ladder alone. It seemed to bounce just as much as before. Each rung I climbed was a victory that set me one foot closer to a lonesome death.

Eye level with the top rung, I found a faded label forbidding anyone to climb above that point. I had to disobey. I needed to climb higher. The top rung passed my chest, then my waist. I stretched and peered.

The gutter was full of transparent, clean water and nothing else. There was no obstruction, no dam of leaves, yet the waterfall continued to spill over the gutter's rim! I felt like crying. There had to be a blockage somewhere... somewhere. Maybe the downspout! I needed to find the downspout!

Looking around, I found it wedged in the corner between the two townhouses. I was too far away to see inside it, though. I balanced my weight on the top rung of the ladder and spread my body against the shingles, using their friction to keep me from sliding off the roof.

I moved an inch to the right. The ladder objected. I moved a half-inch more. The ladder "popped" beneath my feet. I froze, sick with panic.

Then I heard a voice above the din of the storm – a tiny voice, a three-year old girl's voice, singing.

"It-sy bit-sy spi-der climbed up the wa-ter spout…"

I couldn't make it stop. The song got louder and more insistent. "Shut up!" I shouted into the rain. The singing softened but the simple little tune dug into the outer edge of all my thoughts.

I pressed my hands firmly against the shingles, carefully pulling my body over using just my fingers. I was on the final edge of balance. One more inch, just one more inch was all I needed.

I craned my neck over the roof's edge and finally saw into the downspout. Inside was the most terrifying thing I had ever seen.

The drain was clogged with a partially submerged wasps' nest.

"A-long came the rain and washed the spi-der out…"

The singing got louder. I knew wasps could live underwater. I also knew they probably wouldn't like it, leaving the nest populated with stinging bugs in a bad mood.

I needed gloves that I didn't have. I had a pair somewhere inside, but I knew I would never be able to climb the ladder again once my feet tasted solid ground. I had to clear the obstruction immediately. I was only going to get one chance to do this. I was going to have to reach in and grab the nest with my bare hand.

Whatever wasps were left clinging to it would react instantly. I'd have to hold onto to the nest tightly and get it out of the gutter. I'd have to ignore the pain. I'd have to control my reflexes. I didn't know whether it would be possible, but I did know I couldn't afford to jump or jerk or even flinch when the stinging started.

I tried to swallow but my mouth was dry in spite of the torrential rain. Precious seconds ticked by. I was wasting time. The three-year old girl was screaming the lyrics into my ears.

"IT-sy BIT-sy SPI-der..."

I clamped my eyes shut and stabbed my hand into the drain. I felt the nest enter my palm and I squeezed HARD, forcing my hand to hang on, hang on just a little longer. Another second ticked slowly by. PULL! I told my hand.

I jerked the nest free of the gutter and let it fall onto the lawn, far below. Unclogged, water rushed down the spout. The deluge into the basement window stopped.

I must have been stung ten or twenty times. I marveled at the complete absence of pain, and then remembered I was still leaning WAY too far out. I held my breath and inched back to the safety of the top rung. The little girl was quiet at last.

My wife came out of the townhouse and stooped over the fallen nest. She held it up for me to look at and her lips moved. I couldn't hear what she said. The rain was too loud.

I hurried down, skipping rungs as I dropped. "What?" I yelled, jumping off the last rung.

"Ball," she answered. She held something out for me to see.

"That's a tennis ball," I said.

"Yeah. No big deal." She tossed the rotten ball onto the ground.

I looked around the lawn for the wasp's nest I had dropped. I had risked my life to pull it out of the gutter. I had seen it land. The lawn was empty except for an old, wet tennis ball.

When the rain stopped, I put the ladder away. I never used it again. I was disappointed at having nothing but a weather-beaten ball as a trophy, but I knew I had crossed a line that afternoon. Mizroo watched with curious amusement as I swaggered around the house until well after dark, wondering why I kept humming the same silly tune.

OTHER BOOKS BY JON ETHEREDGE

*** The Incredibly Normal Adventures of RoosterBoots

*** Abigail Dare

*** Dream Talker

Made in the USA
Middletown, DE
26 August 2015